PENGUIN CLASSICS
Maigret and the Ghost

'Extraordinary masterpieces of the twentieth century'
– John Banville

'A brilliant writer'   – India Knight

'Intense atmosphere and resonant detail . . . make Simenon's
fiction remarkably like life'   – Julian Barnes

'A truly wonderful writer . . . marvellously readable – lucid,
simple, absolutely in tune with the world he creates'
– Muriel Spark

'Few writers have ever conveyed with such a sure touch, the
bleakness of human life'   – A. N. Wilson

'Compelling, remorseless, brilliant'   – John Gray

'A writer of genius, one whose simplicity of language creates
indelible images that the florid stylists of our own day can
only dream of'   – *Daily Mail*

'The mysteries of the human personality are revealed in all
their disconcerting complexity'   – Anita Brookner

'One of the greatest writers of our time' – *The Sunday Times*

'I love reading Simenon. He makes me think of Chekhov'
– William Faulkner

'One of the great psychological novelists of this century'
– *Independent*

'The greatest of all, the most genuine novelist we have had
in literature'   – André Gide

'Simenon ought to be spoken of in the same breath as
Camus, Beckett and Kafka'   – *Independent on Sunday*

GEORGES SIMENON

Maigret and the Ghost

Translated by ROS SCHWARTZ

PENGUIN BOOKS

PENGUIN CLASSICS

UK | USA | Canada | Ireland | Australia
India | New Zealand | South Africa

Penguin Books is part of the Penguin Random House group of companies
whose addresses can be found at global.penguinrandomhouse.com.

Penguin
Random House
UK

First published in French as *Maigret et le fantome* by Presses de la Cité, 1964
This translation first published 2018
003

Set in 12.5/15 pt Dante MT Std
Typeset by Jouve (UK), Milton Keynes
Printed and bound in Great Britain by Clays Ltd, Elcograf S.p.A.

ISBN: 978–0–241–30403–7

www.greenpenguin.co.uk

Contents

1. Inspector Lognon's Strange Nights and Solange's Ailments

It was just after one o'clock in the morning when the light went out in Maigret's office. Puffy-eyed with tiredness, Maigret pushed open the door to the inspectors' office, where young Lapointe and Bonfils were on duty.

'Good night, boys,' he grunted.

In the vast corridor the cleaning women were sweeping the floor, and he gave them a little wave. As always at that hour, there was a draught, and the staircase he descended in the company of Janvier was damp and freezing.

This was mid-November and it had rained all day. Maigret hadn't left the stiflingly hot atmosphere of his office since eight o'clock the previous morning. Before crossing the courtyard, he turned up the collar of his overcoat.

'Shall I drop you off somewhere?'

A taxi, ordered by telephone, was stationed in front of the entrance to Quai des Orfèvres.

'At any Métro station, chief.'

It was pouring down, the rain bouncing off the pavements. Janvier got out of the car at Châtelet.

'Good night, chief.'

'Good night, Janvier.'

It was a moment like so many others they had shared, and they both felt the same slightly weary sense of satisfaction.

I

A few minutes later, Maigret noiselessly climbed the stairs up to his apartment in Boulevard Richard-Lenoir, fumbling in his pocket for his key. He turned it quietly in the lock, and almost at once heard Madame Maigret stir in bed.

'Is that you?'

She had asked that same question sleepily hundreds, if not thousands, of times when he came home in the middle of the night, groping for the bedside light and then getting up in her nightdress and glancing at her husband to gauge his mood.

'Is it over?'

'Yes.'

'Did the boy talk in the end?'

He nodded.

'Are you hungry? Do you want me to make you something to eat?'

He had hung up his wet overcoat on the coat-stand and was loosening his tie.

'Is there any beer in the refrigerator?'

He had almost stopped the car at Place de la République to down a beer in a brasserie that was still open.

'Did it turn out to be what you thought?'

A run-of-the-mill affair, as much as a case implicating several people can be described as run-of-the-mill. The newspapers had dubbed them 'The Bike Gang'.

The first time, two motorbikes had pulled up in front of a jeweller's in Rue de Rennes in broad daylight. Two men had jumped off one, and a third off the other, their faces masked with red bandanas. All three had dashed into the shop and emerged minutes later, brandishing guns, with jewels and watches snatched from the window and the counter.

In the heat of the moment, the bystanders had been numb with shock, and when motorists eventually reacted and thought to give chase to the thieves, it had caused such a traffic jam that the culprits were able to get away.

'They'll strike again,' Maigret had predicted.

The haul was meagre, because the jeweller's, owned by a widow, only sold cheap goods.

'They wanted to perfect their technique.'

This was the first time that motorbikes had been used in a hold-up.

Maigret was not mistaken, because three days later the scenario was repeated, this time in a luxury jeweller's in Faubourg Saint-Honoré. The result was the same, only this time the bandits had looted jewellery worth several million old francs, two hundred million according to the newspapers, one hundred said the insurance company.

But, as they made their getaway, one of the robbers had lost his bandana and he had been arrested two days later at the locksmith's where he worked, in Rue Saint-Paul.

By that evening all three were behind bars, the eldest aged twenty-two and the youngest, Jean Bauche, nick-named Jeannot, just eighteen.

He was blond, his hair too long, and was the son of a cleaning woman in Rue Saint-Antoine. He too worked in a locksmith's.

'Janvier and I took turns all day,' an irritable Maigret told his wife.

Drinking beer and eating sandwiches.

'Listen, Jeannot. You think you're a tough guy. They had you believe you were. But it was neither you nor your little friends who planned those robberies. There's someone behind you, someone who orchestrated the whole thing, taking care not to get his hands dirty. He was released from Fresnes two months ago and isn't keen to go back to prison. Admit he was at the scene, in a stolen car, and that he covered your getaway by faking a clumsy manoeuvre and holding up the traffic . . .'

Maigret undressed, taking the occasional sip of beer, bringing his wife up to date in terse sentences.

'Those kids are the toughest . . . They have a very strong code of honour instilled into them . . .'

He'd had three repeat offenders arrested, including a certain Gaston Nouveau. As was to be expected, he had a watertight alibi; two people had stated that, at the time of the heist, he'd been in a bar in Avenue des Ternes.

For hours, the questioning had stalled. Plump Victor Sidon, nicknamed 'Granny', the eldest of the three bikers, looked at Maigret contemptuously. Saugier, known as 'Banger', cried, swearing he knew nothing.

'Janvier and I concentrated our efforts on young Bauche. We had his mother brought in, and she begged him:

'"Talk, Jeannot! You can see that these gentlemen aren't after you. They know you let yourself be led astray . . ."'

Twenty unpleasant hours, relentlessly pushing a kid to the limits of human resistance. It wasn't pleasant either to see him suddenly crack.

'"All right! I'll tell you everything. Yes, it was Nouveau

4

who approached us at the Lotus and who got us involved in the racket . . ."'

A little bar in Rue Saint-Antoine, where young boys and girls went to listen to the jukeboxes.

'"Because of you, when I get out of prison, he'll have me killed by his friends . . ."'

That was all! Another day done. Maigret went to bed, his head throbbing.

'What time do you have to be at the office?'

'Nine o'clock.'

'Can't you sleep in a little?'

'Wake me up at eight.'

There was no transition to speak of. He didn't feel as if he'd slept. No sooner had he closed his eyes, it seemed, than the doorbell was ringing and his wife slipping out of bed to go and answer it.

There was whispering in the hallway. He thought he recognized the voice, told himself he must be dreaming and buried his head under the pillow.

Again, his wife's footsteps padding towards the bed. Was she going to go back to sleep? Had someone rung the wrong bell? No. She touched his shoulder, drew back the curtains and, without needing to open his eyes, he was aware that it was daylight. He asked in a slurred voice:

'What time is it?'

'Seven o'clock.'

'Is someone here?'

'Lapointe's waiting for you in the dining room.'

'What does he want?'

'I don't know. Stay in bed for a minute while I make you a cup of coffee.'

Why was his wife talking to him as if she'd just been given bad news? Why had she been loath to answer his question? It was a filthy grey day and the rain was still coming down.

Initially Maigret thought that Jean Bauche, thrown into a panic by his confession, had hanged himself in his police cell. He got up without waiting for his coffee, pulled on his trousers, ran a comb through his hair and opened the dining-room door, still groggy from too deep a sleep.

Lapointe stood by the window, wearing a black overcoat and holding a dark-coloured hat, his cheeks covered in stubble after a night on duty.

Maigret merely gave him a quizzical look.

'I apologize for waking you up so early, chief . . . Something happened last night, to someone you're fond of . . .'

'Janvier?'

'No . . . Not someone from Quai des Orfèvres . . .'

Madame Maigret brought in two large cups of coffee.

'Lognon . . .'

'Is he dead?'

'Seriously wounded. He was taken to Bichat and Monsieur Mingault, the consultant, has been operating on him for the last three hours . . . I didn't want to come sooner, or telephone you, because, after the day you'd had yesterday, you needed some rest . . . Besides, at first, they didn't think there was much chance that he'd live . . .'

'What happened to him?'

'Two bullets, one in the stomach, the other just below the shoulder.'

'Where?'

'Avenue Junot, on the pavement.'

'Was he alone?'

'Yes. For the time being, it's his colleagues from the eighteenth arrondissement who are investigating.'

Maigret sipped his coffee without experiencing the usual satisfaction.

'I thought you'd want to be there if he regains consciousness. The car's downstairs . . .'

'Do they know anything about the attack?'

'Almost nothing. They don't even know what he was doing in Avenue Junot. A concierge heard the shots and called the emergency services. A bullet went through her shutter, smashed the windowpane and lodged itself in the wall above her bed.'

'I'll get dressed.'

He went into the bathroom while Madame Maigret set the table for breakfast and Lapointe, having removed his overcoat, waited.

Inspector Lognon didn't belong to Quai des Orfèvres, even though he was keen to, but Maigret had worked with him often, almost every time there was a major case in the eighteenth arrondissement.

He was a civvy, as they said, one of the twenty plainclothes inspectors whose office was in the Montmartre town hall, on the corner of Rue Ordener and Rue du Mont-Cenis.

Some called him Inspector Hard-Done-By because of

his sullen expression. But Maigret called him Inspector Luckless, and it did indeed seem as if poor old Lognon had a talent for attracting misfortune.

Short and scrawny, he had a permanent cold which gave him a red nose and the watery eyes of a drunkard, even though he was probably the soberest man in the police force.

He was afflicted with a sick wife, who dragged herself from her bed to an armchair by the window. When he was off duty, Lognon had to manage the housework, the shopping and the cooking. He could just about afford to pay a woman to come once a week to do the heavy cleaning.

On four occasions he had sat the Police Judiciaire entrance exam, and he'd failed each time because of careless mistakes, whereas he was in fact an outstanding police officer, a sort of bloodhound who, once on a trail, would not give up. Obstinate. Meticulous. The type who could immediately smell something suspicious passing someone in the street.

'Do they hope to save him?'

'At Bichat they reckon he has a thirty per cent chance, apparently.'

For a man nicknamed Inspector Luckless, that was not encouraging.

'Has he been able to speak?'

Maigret, his wife and Lapointe ate the croissants which the baker's boy had just left outside the door.

'His colleagues didn't tell me, and I didn't want to press them.'

Lognon wasn't the only one to suffer from an inferiority complex. Most of the neighbourhood inspectors coveted a post at Quai des Orfèvres and, when they had an interesting case likely to make the headlines, they hated the 'big boys' taking it away from them.

'Let's go!' sighed Maigret, putting on his overcoat, which was still damp.

His gaze met his wife's, and he understood that she wanted to speak to him, guessing that the same idea had just occurred to both of them.

'Do you expect to be back for lunch?'

'It's unlikely.'

'In that case, don't you think . . . ?'

She was thinking of Madame Lognon, helpless and alone at home.

'Get dressed quickly! We'll drop you off at Place Constantin-Pecqueur.'

The Lognons had lived there for twenty years, in a red-brick apartment building with yellow bricks surrounding the windows. Maigret had never been able to remember the street number.

Lapointe took the wheel of the little Police Judiciaire car. This was the second time in so many years that Madame Maigret had got into one of these with her husband.

They drove past crammed buses. On the pavements, people walked fast, leaning forward, clutching their umbrellas, which the wind was trying to snatch from their hands.

They reached Montmartre, Rue Caulaincourt.

'It's here . . .'

In the middle of the square was a stone couple, one of the woman's breasts emerging from the folds of her robe, and the statue was black on the side exposed to the rain.

'Telephone me at the office. I hope to be there by late morning.'

One case was barely over when another was beginning, about which he knew nothing yet. He was fond of Lognon. Often, in his official reports, he had highlighted his merits, even crediting him with successes he personally had achieved. But it hadn't helped. Inspector Luckless!

'To Bichat first . . .'

A staircase. Corridors. Rows of beds glimpsed through open doors, the gaze of their occupants following them as they passed.

They were sent the wrong way and had to go back down to the courtyard and up another staircase before reaching, at last, a door marked 'Surgery'. It was being guarded by an inspector from the thirteenth arrondissement whom they knew, a certain Créac, who had an unlit cigarette dangling from his mouth.

'I think you'd better put out your pipe, inspector. There's a dragon here who'll go for you the way she did me when I tried to light my cigarette.'

Nurses went past with bedpans, pitchers, trays of phials and nickel instruments.

'Is he still in there?'

It was eight forty-five.

'They set to work on him at four o'clock . . .'

'You don't have any news?'

'No . . . I tried to inquire at this office on the left, but the old witch . . .'

It was the office of the matron, whom Créac had called the dragon. Maigret knocked on the door. A disagreeable voice bade him enter.

'What is it?'

'I apologize for disturbing you, madame. I am the head of the Crime Squad at the Police Judiciaire . . .'

The woman's frosty glare seemed to say:

'So what?'

'I'd like to know whether you have any news of the inspector who's being operated on at the moment.'

'I'll have some when he's out of surgery. All I can tell you is that he's not dead, because the consultant hasn't come out . . .'

'Was he able to speak when he was brought in?'

She gave him a withering look for asking such an idiotic question.

'He had lost almost half his blood and we had to give him an emergency transfusion.'

'When do you think he's likely to regain consciousness?'

'You'll have to ask Monsieur Mingault.'

'If you have a private room, I'd be grateful if you would reserve it for him. It is important. An inspector will keep watch at his bedside.'

She pricked up her ears because the operating-theatre door had just opened and a man had appeared in the corridor, a skullcap on his head and a bloodstained apron over his white coat.

'Monsieur Mingault, this is someone who—'

'Detective Chief Inspector Maigret.'

'Pleased to meet you.'

'Is he alive?'

'For the time being . . . Barring any complications, I hope to save him.'

His forehead was beaded with sweat, and his eyes betrayed his exhaustion.

'One more thing . . . It is important for him to be put in a private room . . .'

'See to that, Madame Drasse . . . Excuse me.'

He strode towards his office. The door opened again. A nurse was pushing a gurney on which the form of a body could be made out beneath the sheet. That of Lognon, stiff and pale, with only the top half of his face visible.

'Take him to 218, Bernard.'

'Yes, madame.'

She followed the gurney, Maigret, Lapointe and Créac behind her. In the wan light coming from the high windows, they walked past wards lined with beds. It was like being in a bad dream.

A junior doctor came out of the operating theatre and joined the mournful procession.

'Are you family?'

'No . . . Detective Chief Inspector Maigret.'

'Oh! It's you?'

He darted him a curious look, as if to reassure himself that Maigret resembled his mental image of him.

'Monsieur Mingault says there's a chance he'll pull through . . .'

This was a world apart, where voices didn't sound the same as elsewhere and questions did not find answers.

'If he told you so—'

'You have no idea how long it will take him to come round?'

Was Maigret's question so ridiculous that they had to gaze at him in that way? The matron stopped the police officers in front of the door.

'No. Not now.'

They had to settle the wounded patient in, probably administer treatment, because two nurses brought in equipment, including an oxygen tent.

'Wait in the corridor if you must, although I don't like that. There are visiting times.'

Maigret glanced at his watch.

'I think I'll leave you, Créac. Try to be there when he regains consciousness. If he's able to talk, note down exactly what he says.'

No, he didn't feel humiliated. All the same, he felt uncomfortable because he wasn't used to being brushed off like that. Here his renown did not impress people for whom life and death meant something different to what it did to the average person.

Out in the courtyard he was relieved to be able to light his pipe while Lapointe lit a cigarette.

'As for you, you'd better go to bed. Just drop me at the town hall of the eighteenth arrondissement first.

'Won't you let me stay with you, chief?'

'You spent the night—'

'At my age, you know . . .'

They were just around the corner. In the inspectors' office, they found three plainclothes officers hunched over their typewriters writing reports, like conscientious clerks.

'Hello, gentlemen ... Which one of you is up to date ... ?'

He knew them too, if not by name, then at least by sight, and all three had risen to their feet.

'All of us and no one ...'

'Has someone been to talk to Madame Lognon?'

'Durantel's taking care of it.'

There were wet footprints on the floor and the air smelled of stale cigarette smoke.

'Was Lognon on a case?'

They exchanged hesitant glances. Finally one of them, a short, plump officer, began:

'That's precisely what we were wondering ... You know Lognon, sir ... When he was following up a lead he would sometimes behave mysteriously ... It wasn't unusual for him to work on a case for weeks without talking to us about it.'

Because poor Lognon was used to others getting the credit instead of him!

'He'd been acting secretive for at least a fortnight, sometimes coming back to the office with the air of someone who's planning a big surprise ...'

'He didn't give any hints?'

'No. Except that he nearly always chose to be on night duty.'

'Does anyone know which sector he was working in?'

'The patrols spotted him several times in Avenue Junot, not far from the place where he was attacked . . . but not recently . . . He would leave the office at around nine p.m. and come back at around three or four a.m . . . Some nights, he didn't come back at all . . .'

'He didn't keep a written record?'

'I checked the log book. He simply wrote "nothing to report".'

'Have you got men at the scene?'

'Three, led by Chinquier.'

'The press?'

'It's hard to keep an attack on a police inspector from them . . . Don't you want to see the superintendent?'

'Not now.'

Maigret had Lapointe drive him to Avenue Junot. The trees were shedding their last leaves, which were plastered to the damp pavements. It was still raining, but that didn't stop around fifty people from gathering halfway down the avenue.

Uniformed officers had cordoned off a square of pavement in front of a four-storey apartment building. When Maigret alighted from the car and had to push his way through the curious onlookers and the umbrellas, the photographers caught sight of him.

'One more, inspector . . . Take a few steps forward into the crowd . . .'

He glared at them in the same way that the matron had glared at him at Bichat. On the area of empty pavement, the rain hadn't been enough to wash away a pool of blood which was slowly being diluted, and, since it wasn't possible to draw with chalk, the police had formed the outline of a body as best they could using twigs.

Inspector Deliot, from the eighteenth-arrondissement police station, removed his sopping hat to greet Maigret.

'Chinquier is with the concierge, inspector. He was the first on the scene.'

Maigret walked into the old-fashioned but very clean and well-maintained building and pushed open the glass door of the lodge just as Inspector Chinquier was putting his notebook back in his pocket.

'I thought you'd come. I was surprised not to see anyone from Quai des Orfèvres.'

'I dropped into Bichat first.'

'The surgery?'

'It seems to have been successful. The consultant thinks there's a chance he'll pull through.'

The lodge too was clean and tidy. The concierge, who must have been around forty-five, was an affable woman with pleasing curves.

'Have a seat, gentlemen . . . I've just told the inspector everything I know . . . Look at the floor . . .'

The green linoleum was strewn with shards of glass from the smashed windowpane.

'And here . . .'

She pointed to a hole, about a metre above the bed at the back of the room.

'Were you alone at the time?'

'Yes. My husband is a night porter at Le Palace, Avenue des Champs-Élysées, and doesn't get home until eight in the morning.'

'Where is he at the moment?'

'In the kitchen.'

She pointed to a closed door.

'He's trying to rest because he'll have to go back to work this evening, in spite of all this.'

'I presume, Chinquier, that you have asked all the necessary questions. Please don't be annoyed if I ask some myself as well.'

'Do you need me?'

'Not right away.'

'In that case I'll go upstairs for a minute . . .'

Maigret frowned, wondering where he was going, but didn't press the matter, not wishing to offend the neighbourhood inspector.

'Apologies, madame . . .'

'Madame Sauget. The residents call me Angèle.'

'Do please sit down.'

'I'm so used to being on my feet!'

She went over to draw the curtain which hid the bed during the day, turning the room into a little sitting room.

'You don't want anything to drink? A cup of coffee?'

'No thank you. So last night, you were in bed . . .'

'Yes. I heard a voice saying:

'"Door, please . . ."'

'Do you know what time that was?'

'My alarm clock has phosphorescent numbers. It was twenty past two.'

'Was it one of your residents on their way out?'

'No. It was that gentleman . . .'

She spoke with the awkwardness of someone forced to be indiscreet.

'What gentleman?'

'The one who was attacked . . .'

Maigret and Lapointe looked at one another in amazement.

'Do you mean Inspector Lognon?'

She nodded, adding:

'We have to tell the police everything, don't we? I don't usually talk about my residents, about what they do or who visits them. Their private life is none of my business, but after what's happened . . .'

'Have you known the inspector long?'

'Yes, for years . . . Ever since my husband and I have lived here . . . but I didn't know his name. I saw him go past and I knew he was in the police, because he came into the lodge several times to carry out identity checks . . . He's not very talkative . . .'

'How did you get to know him better?'

'When he started seeing the young lady on the fourth floor . . .'

This time Maigret was left speechless. As for Lapointe, he was completely stunned. Policemen aren't necessarily saints. Maigret was not unaware that in his own department, some officers did not shy away from extramarital affairs.

But Lognon! . . . That Hard-Done-By should pay nocturnal visits to a young lady, two hundred metres from his own home!

'Are you sure it's the same man?'

'He's quite recognizable, isn't he?'

'How long has . . . has he been going up to see this person?'

'About ten days . . .'

'So one night, I presume, he came home with her?'

'Yes.'

'Did he hide his face as he passed the lodge?'

'I think so.'

'Did he come back often?'

'Almost every night . . .'

'Did he leave very late?'

'Initially, I mean the first three or four days, he left just after midnight . . . Then he stayed later, until two or three in the morning . . .'

'What's this woman's name?'

'Marinette . . . Marinette Augier . . . A very pretty girl of twenty-five, a nice young lady . . .'

'Is she in the habit of receiving gentleman visitors?'

'I think I can answer, because she's never made a secret of her behaviour . . . For a year, she received two or three visits a week from a good-looking young man she told me was her fiancé . . .'

'Did he spend the night with her?'

'You'll find out sooner or later . . . Yes . . . And when he stopped coming, I thought she looked sad . . . One morning, when she came to collect her post, I asked her whether the engagement was off, and she replied:

'"Don't talk to me about it ever again, Angèle. Men aren't worth crying over . . ."'

'She can't have fretted over him for long, because she soon recovered her good spirits . . . She's a very jolly girl, robust . . .'

'Does she work?'

'She's a beautician, from what she told me, in a salon on Avenue Matignon . . . That explains why she's always so well groomed, tastefully dressed—'

'What about her boyfriend?'

'The fiancé who never came back? He was around thirty. I don't know what he did for a living. I only know his first name. I called him Monsieur Henri, the name he gave when he passed the lodge at night—'

'When did they break up?'

'Last winter, around Christmas time . . .'

'So, for nearly a year, this young lady . . . What did you say her name is . . . Marinette?'

'Marinette Augier . . .'

'For nearly a year, then, she didn't have any visitors?'

'Only her brother, from time to time. He lives in the suburbs with his wife and their three children.'

'A couple of weeks ago, she came home one night accompanied by Inspector Lognon?'

'Like I told you.'

'And since then, he's been back every day?'

'Except Sunday, unless I didn't see him come in or leave.'

'He never came during the day?'

'No. But you've just reminded me of a detail. One night he arrived at around nine o'clock, as usual. I ran after him before he started going up the stairs to say:

'"Marinette's not home."

'"I know," he replied, "she's at her brother's . . ."

'He went upstairs all the same, with no explanation, so I assume she'd given him the key . . .'

Maigret now understood why Inspector Chinquier had gone upstairs.

'Is Mademoiselle Augier home at the moment?'

'No.'

'Did she go to work?'

'I don't know, but when I wanted to tell her what had happened, and break it to her gently—'

'At what time?'

'After phoning the police . . .'

'So before three o'clock in the morning?'

'Yes . . . I said to myself that she must have heard the shots . . . All the residents did . . . Some were leaning out of their windows, others came down in their dressing gowns to find out what was going on . . .

'On the pavement, it was not a pretty sight . . . So I ran upstairs and knocked on her door . . . No one answered . . . I went in and found the apartment empty . . .'

She looked at Maigret with a certain smugness, as if to say:

'You might have come across some strange things in the course of your career, but admit that you weren't expecting this!'

It was true. Maigret and Lapointe could only exchange nonplussed glances. Maigret was thinking that meanwhile his wife was with Madame Lognon, whose first name was Solange, consoling her and probably doing her housework!

'Do you think she left the building when he did?'

'I'm positive she didn't. I have keen hearing and I'm sure that only one person, a man—'

'Did he shout his name in passing?'

'No. He was in the habit of yelling: "Fourth!" I recognized his voice. Besides, he was the only one who used that word.'

'Could she have left before him?'

'No. I only opened the door once last night, at half past eleven, to the people from the third floor who came back from the cinema.'

'Could she have gone out after the shooting?'

'That's the only explanation. When I saw the body on the pavement, I raced in here to telephone the emergency services . . . I wasn't sure whether to close the main door . . . I didn't dare . . . It felt as if it would be abandoning the poor man—'

'Did you lean over him to find out whether he was dead?'

'It was hard, because I hate the sight of blood, but I did . . .'

'Was he conscious?'

'I don't know . . .'

'He didn't say anything?'

'His lips moved . . . I could tell he wanted to speak . . . I thought I made out a word, but I must have got it wrong, because it makes no sense . . . Maybe he was delirious—'

'What word?'

'Ghost . . .'

She blushed, as if she were afraid that Maigret and Lapointe would laugh at her or accuse her of making things up.

2. Lunch at Chez Manière

It was as if the man had chosen that particular moment for dramatic effect. Maybe he'd been listening at the door? The word *ghost* had barely been uttered when the knob turned, the door opened a fraction and a head appeared while the rest of the body remained unseen.

His face was pale, his features drawn, his eyelids and mouth drooping, and it took Maigret a few seconds to realize that what gave the newcomer his mournful expression was the absence of dentures.

'Aren't you asleep, Raoul?'

And, as if it were necessary, she introduced the man:

'My husband, inspector.'

Much older than her, he was wearing an unsightly purple dressing gown over his pyjamas.

Behind his desk at Le Palace, in his gold-trimmed livery, he must have cut a fine figure, but here, unshaven, his body weary, with the scowl of someone who can't get to sleep, he was both ridiculous and pathetic.

Holding a cup of coffee, he vaguely greeted Maigret, then his gaze turned to the lace curtains on the other side of which dark shapes were still clustered in the driving rain, despite the police officers' efforts to keep them at bay.

'Is this going to go on for long?' he groaned.

He was being deprived of his much-needed sleep, the

sleep he was entitled to, and from the look on his face, anyone would have thought that he was the real victim.

'Why don't you take one of those pills the doctor prescribed?'

'They give me a stomach ache.'

He sat down in a corner to drink his coffee, his feet bare inside felt slippers, opening his mouth only to sigh during the rest of the interview.

'Madame, I'd like you to try and remember what happened, almost second by second, from the moment when you were asked to open the door.'

Why this delectable woman had married a man at least twenty years her senior was none of his business, and she probably hadn't seen him without his dentures at the time.

'I heard: "Door-pull, please."'

'And the voice, which I recognized, shouted:'

'"Fourth!"'

'As I've already told you, I automatically glanced at the clock. It's a habit. The time was twenty past two. I reached out to press the button, because nowadays there isn't a door-pull any more, but an electric button that opens the door.

'Just then I thought I heard the sound of an engine, as if a car was parked not right outside but further along, with the motor still running. I even said to myself that it was probably the Hardsins – a couple who live in the next building who often come home in the small hours.

'All that only lasted a few seconds. I also heard Monsieur Lognon's footsteps in the corridor. Then the door slammed. Immediately afterwards, the sound of the engine grew louder, the car pulled away and a shot rang out, then another, and a third . . .'

'They might as well have taken aim at the lodge itself with that last one, because it hit the shutter, broke the window, and there was a strange sound above my head . . .'

'Did the car carry on driving? Are you sure there was a car?'

The husband looked from one to the other, his head bowed, stirring the spoon in his cup.

'I'm positive. The street is on a slope. To drive up it, cars accelerate. That one went full throttle in the direction of Rue Norvins.'

'You don't recall hearing a shout?'

'No. At first I stayed put because I was frightened. But women always want to know, to find out what's going on. I switched on the light, grabbed my dressing gown and rushed into the corridor.'

'Was the front door closed?'

'I told you. I heard it slam. I pressed my ear to it and could only hear the rain. So I opened it a fraction and I saw the body barely two metres from the doorway.'

'Facing the top of the street or the bottom?'

'More as if he'd been heading towards Rue Caulaincourt. The poor man was clutching his stomach with both hands and blood was streaming over his fingers. His open eyes were staring at me.'

'You leaned over and that's when you heard, or thought you heard, the word *ghost*?'

'I'd swear that that's what he whispered. Windows opened. Residents don't have their own telephones and have to use the one in the lodge. Two of them who've applied for a phone have been on the waiting list for over a year.

'I came back inside and looked up the emergency services number in the directory. You should know these things, but you don't think about it, especially in a quiet building like ours . . .'

'Was the light on in the corridor?'

'No. Only in my lodge. The operator on the other end asked me questions, thinking it was a hoax, so it took a while . . .'

The telephone was wall-mounted. From where it was positioned, you could see into the corridor.

'Residents came down . . . I told you all that . . . After hanging up, I thought of Marinette and I dashed up to the fourth floor—'

'Thank you. May I use your phone?'

Maigret called the Police Judiciaire.

'Hello! Is that you, Lucas? You must have found a note from Lapointe about Lognon . . . No, I'm not at the hospital any more . . . They don't know if he'll pull through yet . . . I'm at Avenue Junot . . . I'd like you to go over to Bichat . . . Yes, yourself preferably . . . Put on your most official manner, because those people don't much care for outsiders . . .

'Try to see the junior doctor who was present during surgery, because Monsieur Mingault's probably unavailable at this hour . . . I presume they found the bullet, two most likely . . . Yes . . . I'd like to have as many details as possible while I'm waiting for the official report . . . And take the bullets to the laboratory . . .'

In the past, this job was given to a civilian expert, Gastinne Renette, but now they had a ballistics expert in the Police Judiciaire laboratories, in the eaves of the Palais de Justice.

'I'll see you soon or early this afternoon . . .'

Maigret turned to Lapointe.

'Do you really not want to go home to bed?'

'I'm not sleepy, chief.'

The night porter from Le Palace shot him a look that was a mixture of envy and disapproval.

'In that case, go over to Avenue Matignon. There can't be so many beauty salons that you won't be able to find the one where Marinette Augier works . . . It's highly unlikely she'll be there . . . Try to discover as much as you can about her . . .'

'Understood, chief.'

'And I'll go upstairs . . .'

Maigret was a little annoyed not to have thought of the bullets when he was at the hospital, but this was no ordinary investigation. It was as if, because it involved Lognon, it had taken on a less professional character.

At Bichat, he had been thinking first and foremost about the inspector and had allowed himself to be intimidated by the matron, the consultant and the wards where the rows of patients followed him with their eyes.

The building on Avenue Junot had no lift. There was no carpet on the stairs either, but the wooden treads, shiny from wear, were well polished, the handrail smooth. There were two apartments on each floor, and some doors had brass name plates.

On the fourth floor, he pushed the half-open door, crossed a dark hallway and found himself in a living room where Inspector Chinquier was sitting in a floral chintz-covered armchair, smoking his cigarette.

'I was waiting for you . . . Did she tell you everything?'

'Yes.'

'Did she mention the car? . . . That's what I found most striking . . . Look at this . . .'

He stood up and pulled from his pocket three shiny cartridge cases which he'd wrapped in a piece of newspaper.

'We found them in the street . . . If the gun was fired from a moving car, which is likely, the shooter had his arm out of the door . . . You'll notice that it's a 7.63 . . .'

Chinquier was a conscientious police officer who knew his job.

'The weapon was probably an automatic Mauser pistol. A heavy weapon that can't be slipped into a handbag or a trouser pocket . . . You see what I mean? . . . It appears to be the work of a professional who had at least one accomplice at the wheel, because he didn't shoot while driving . . . Generally, a jealous lover doesn't enlist his friends to help him kill his rival . . . What's more, he aimed at the stomach . . .'

It is more certain than aiming at the chest, because a man rarely survives when his intestines have been perforated in a dozen places by a high-calibre bullet.

'Have you looked around the apartment?'

'I'd like you to see for yourself.'

This investigation presented another distinctive

characteristic that made Maigret feel uncomfortable. It had been launched by the neighbourhood police force. Now, although they readily laughed at Lognon when he was on both feet, it was still their colleague who had been gunned down. Under the circumstances, Maigret could hardly sideline them and take over the case on his own.

'This room's not bad, is it?'

With a little sunshine, it would be even more pleasant. The walls were a vibrant yellow and the floor varnished, with a light-yellow rug in the centre. The modern furniture had been tastefully chosen, creating a lounge-dining room, and there was both a television and a record player.

On the central table, Maigret had immediately noticed an electric coffee maker, a cup with coffee dregs, a sugar bowl and a bottle of brandy.

'Only one cup . . .' he grunted. 'You haven't touched it, Chinquier? You should call Quai des Orfèvres and ask them to send the lab team.'

He did not remove his overcoat and had put his hat back on. One of the armchairs was facing the window, close to a pedestal table, and an ashtray contained seven or eight cigarette ends.

Two doors opened into the living room. The first led to the kitchen, which was clean and tidy and resembled one of those model showroom kitchens rather than the kind usually found in old Parisian apartment buildings.

The second door led to the bedroom. The bed was unmade. The pillow, the only pillow, still had the dent made by one head.

A pale-blue silk dressing gown had been slung over the

back of a chair, a woman's pyjama jacket of the same colour lay on the floor, and the bottoms at the foot of a wardrobe.

Chinquier was already coming back up.

'I got Moers on the phone. He's sending the team over right away. Have you had a chance to look around? Have you opened the wardrobe?'

'Not yet . . .'

He opened it. Five dresses on hangers, a fur-trimmed winter coat and two suits, one beige and the other navy blue.

Suitcases were stacked on the top shelf.

'You see what I mean? It doesn't look as if she took any luggage. In the chest of drawers, you'll find her underwear, neatly arranged.

The window had a view over part of Paris but mainly, especially today, of the grey sky from which the rain continued to pelt down. Past the bed, a door led into the bathroom, where nothing was missing either, not the toothbrush or the beauty creams.

Judging from her apartment, Marinette Augier was a person with taste, who spent a good deal of time at home and liked her comfort.

'I forgot to ask the concierge whether she cooked or whether she ate in restaurants,' admitted Maigret.

'I did. She nearly always eats here . . .'

The refrigerator contained half a cold chicken, butter, cheese, fruit, two bottles of beer and a bottle of mineral water. In the bedroom, on the bedside table, another bottle had been opened.

On the same bedside table, Maigret was more interested in the ashtray, which contained two lipstick-stained cigarette butts.

'She smokes Virginia tobacco . . .'

'Whereas in the living room, someone was smoking Gauloises, correct?'

The two men exchanged a look, because the same thing had occurred to both of them.

'Judging by the state of the bed, there are no signs that last night was spent love-making . . .'

Despite the tragedy, it was hard not to smile at the thought of Inspector Hard-Done-By in the arms of a pretty, young beautician.

Had they argued? Had a sulking Lognon taken refuge in the next room, sunk in an armchair and chain-smoked while his mistress was in bed?

Something wasn't right, and Maigret realized, once again, that from the start he had not handled this case with his usual clear-headedness.

'I'm sorry to ask you to go downstairs again, Chinquier, but there's one more question I forgot to ask. I'd like to know whether the concierge found a light on in the living room when she came upstairs.'

'I can tell you. There was a light in the bedroom, whose door was open, but not in the other rooms.'

They went back together into the living room whose full-length windows opened on to a balcony running the entire length of the façade, as is common on the top floor of old apartment buildings in Paris.

Despite the greyness, it was just about possible to make

out the Eiffel Tower, the church bell towers and, on hundreds of roofs glistening in the rain, smoking chimney stacks.

In the early days of his career, Maigret had known Avenue Junot when it was still a building site with only a few apartment blocks amid the patches of wasteland and gardens. A painter had been the first to build a sort of private mansion, which at the time was considered very modern.

Others had followed his example – a novelist, an opera singer – and Avenue Junot had become a fashionable address.

Through the French windows, Maigret could see several private residences which had ended up adjoining each other. From its style, the one opposite must have been around fifteen years old, and it had two storeys.

Did it belong to a painter, as the almost entirely glazed second floor seemed to suggest? Dark curtains were drawn, leaving only a thirty- to forty-centimetre gap between them.

Had Maigret been asked what he was thinking about, he would have had difficulty answering. He was taking it all in. In no particular order. Randomly. At times he looked outside, at times inside the apartment, knowing that at a given moment, some images would connect up and make sense.

A noise was heard coming from the street, heavy footsteps on the stairs, voices, banging. The team from Criminal Records had arrived with all their equipment, and Moers had taken the trouble to come in person.

'Where's the body?' he asked, his blue eyes always seeming a little startled behind the thick lenses of his glasses.

'There's no body. Didn't Chinquier tell you?'

'I was in such a rush . . .' apologized the latter.

'It's Lognon, who was shot as he was leaving the building.'

'Is he dead?'

'He's been taken to Bichat. He may pull through. He spent part of the night in this apartment with a woman. I'd like to know if there are any of his fingerprints in the bedroom or only in this room. Take all the prints you can find . . . Are you coming downstairs with me, Chinquier?'

He waited until they were in the corridor downstairs before saying to him quietly:

'It might be useful to question the residents and neighbours. There's not much likelihood anyone was at their window, given the weather at the time of the shooting, but you never know.

'It is also possible that young Marinette took a taxi and, if she did, it won't be hard to find the driver. She probably went down to Place Constantin-Pecqueur, where there are more cars than up on Montmartre . . . You know the area better than me, so do your colleagues . . .'

Shaking Chinquier's hand, he sighed:

'Good luck!'

And he pushed open the glass lodge door. The concierge's husband had decided to go to sleep in his bed because his regular breathing could be heard coming from behind the curtain.

'Do you need anything else?' whispered Angèle Sauget.

'No. I wanted to make a telephone call, but I'll go elsewhere. I'd rather not disturb him.'

'Don't be annoyed with him. When he doesn't get enough rest, he's impossible. I gave him a sleeping tablet, which is beginning to work.'

'If you remember any further details, please do telephone the Police Judiciaire.'

'I'd be surprised, but I will, I promise. If only those journalists and photographers would go away! They're the ones attracting the gawkers.'

'I'll try to move them on.'

As he expected, the minute he stepped outside they mobbed him, despite the police presence.

'Listen, gentlemen, right now, I don't know any more than you do. Inspector Lognon was attacked while on duty by persons unknown . . .'

'On duty?' shouted a mocking voice.

'I said while on duty, and I repeat it. He was severely wounded and was operated on by Monsieur Mingault at Bichat, but he probably won't be able to talk for some hours, if not days.

'In the meantime, we can only surmise. In any case, there's nothing more to see here, but it is possible that, this afternoon at Quai des Orfèvres, I'll have some news for you . . .'

'What was the inspector doing in this building? Is it true that a young woman has disappeared?'

'See you this afternoon!'

'Don't you want to comment?'

'I don't know anything.'

And, his overcoat collar upturned and his hands thrust in his pockets, he walked off down the street. The sound of a few clicks told him he was being photographed, for lack of anything else, and when he looked around, the reporters were beginning to disperse.

In Rue Caulaincourt he went into the first café he saw and ordered a grog, since he'd felt shivery earlier.

'Give me three phone tokens, would you?'

'Three?'

He took a big swig of his grog before going into the telephone booth, and his first call was to the hospital. As anticipated, he was transferred to several departments before he was put through to the matron on the surgery ward.

'No, he's not dead. A junior doctor is with him right now and one of your inspectors is waiting in the corridor. It's still too early to say. That's it! Now another one of your men is coming into my office . . .'

Resigned, he hung up and called Quai des Orfèvres.

'Is Lapointe back?'

'He just tried to reach you at Avenue Junot. I'll put him on.'

Through the glass wall of the booth, Maigret could see the pewter counter, the bar owner in his shirt-sleeves, and two builders being served large glasses of red wine.

'Is that you, chief? I found the beauty salon straight away because it's the only one in Avenue Matignon. It's a luxury establishment, run by a certain Marcellin. The ladies speak very highly of him. Marinette Augier didn't turn up today and her colleagues are surprised because, they say, she's very punctual and hard-working . . .

'She hasn't told anyone about her relationship with Lognon . . . She has a married brother, who lives in Vanves, but no one knows his address . . . He's in insurance, and Marinette occasionally telephoned him at the office . . . The company's called La Fraternelle . . . I looked it up in the phone book . . . It's in Rue Le Peletier . . .

'I didn't want to go there without talking to you first—'

'Is Janvier with you?'

'He's typing out a report.'

'Ask him if it's urgent. I insist you go to bed so that you'll be available when I need you . . .'

A silence at the other end. Then Lapointe's resigned voice:

'He says it's not urgent.'

'Then fill him in. Tell him to go to Rue Le Peletier and see if he can find out where Marinette might be hiding.'

Other customers came into the little café, regulars who were served without having to be asked what they wanted to drink. People had recognized Maigret and were darting inquisitive glances over at the glass telephone booth.

He had to look up Lognon's number. Unsurprisingly, it was Madame Maigret who picked up the phone.

'Where are you?' she asked.

'Shhh! . . . Whatever you do, don't tell her I'm around the corner . . . How is she?'

He understood his wife's hesitation.

'I imagine she's in bed and that she feels worse than her husband?'

'Yes.'

'Have you made her something to eat?'

'After going to the local shops.'

'So you can leave her on her own?'

'She won't be happy!'

'Whether she likes it or not, tell her I need you and come and meet me as quickly as possible at Chez Manière.'

'Are we having lunch together?'

She couldn't believe her ears. Although they sometimes went out to eat on a Saturday evening or a Sunday, they almost never had lunch out together, particularly in the middle of an investigation.

Maigret finished his grog at the bar, the voices around him sounding artificial. That was the price he paid for the unwanted publicity the newspapers gave him, which often hindered his work.

Someone said, without looking at him:

'Is it true that Hard-Done-By was shot by gangsters?'

And another, ominously:

'If they really are gangsters.'

There were rumours in the neighbourhood about the relationship between Lognon and Marinette. Maigret paid and left, with everyone staring after him, and made his way to Chez Manière.

Located next to a flight of stone steps, the restaurant was a favourite haunt of local celebrities and you could still rub shoulders with actresses, writers and painters. It was too early for the regulars and most of the tables were free, with only a handful of customers at the bar.

He removed his wet overcoat and his hat and sank down on to the banquette by the window with a contented sigh.

He had the time to smoke a pipe, a dreamy look in his eyes, before spotting Madame Maigret as she crossed the road, holding her umbrella like a shield.

'It feels funny, meeting you at this restaurant . . . It's at least fifteen years since we last ate here, one evening, after the theatre . . . Do you remember?'

'Yes . . . What will you have?'

He held out the menu.

'I already know that you'll choose the andouillette . . . Can I be a bit extravagant and order cold lobster with mayonnaise?'

They waited until the starter and the Loire wine were on the table. There was no one next to them. The misted-up window made the atmosphere cosy.

'I feel a bit like one of your team . . . When you phone me to say you won't be home for lunch, this is how I picture you, with Lucas or Janvier . . .'

'Unless I'm in my office making do with sandwiches and a beer . . . So tell me . . .'

'I don't want to be unkind . . .'

'Be honest.'

'You've often talked to me about her and her husband . . . He was the one you felt sorry for, and I was close to thinking you were being unfair—'

'And now?'

'I no longer pity her as much, even though it's probably not her fault . . . I found her in bed, and the concierge was there with her, along with an elderly neighbour who sits telling her beads all day long . . . They'd called the doctor because she looked as if she was at death's door . . .'

'Was she surprised at your visit?'

'Do you know what her opening words were?

'"In any case, your husband won't be able to persecute him any more . . . He'll be sorry he never let Charles join Quai des Orfèvres . . ."

'At first, I felt uncomfortable . . . Luckily, the doctor arrived, a calm little old man with a wry expression . . .

'The concierge went downstairs. The old woman followed me into the dining room, still clutching her rosary.

'"Poor woman! We're such fragile creatures! When you think about everything that's going on around us, it makes you afraid to go out into the street . . ."

'I asked her if Madame Lognon was seriously ill and she told me that her legs could barely carry her, and that it was probably her bones . . .'

They couldn't help smiling, both of them relishing the intimacy of this meal in an ambience that was different from that of Boulevard Richard-Lenoir. Madame Maigret especially was thrilled. Her eyes were brighter than usual and her face was flushed as she spoke.

When they ate lunch or dinner at home, it was chiefly Maigret who did the talking, because she had nothing much to tell. This time, she was conscious of being useful to him.

'Does it interest you?'

'A great deal. Go on.'

'When the consultation was over, the doctor signalled to me to follow him into the hallway and we spoke in hushed tones. First of all, he asked me if I was indeed the wife of Detective Chief Inspector Maigret, and he seemed taken aback to find me there.

'I explained . . . Well, you can guess what I said to him . . .

'"I understand your sentiments," he said. "It's very kind of you . . . but let me warn you . . . Without claiming that she has an iron constitution, I can tell you that she is not suffering from any serious illness . . . I've been treating her for ten years . . . and I'm not the only one!

'"She regularly calls on one or another of my colleagues, wanting them at all costs to discover a major ailment . . . But when I talk to her about seeing a psychiatrist or a neurologist, she becomes angry, swearing she's not mad and telling me that I don't know my job . . .

'"Is she disappointed in her marriage? In any case, she's furious at her husband for remaining a mere neighbour-hood inspector . . .

'"So she takes her revenge by passing herself off as sick, forcing him to care for her and do the housework, and making his life impossible.

'"I understand why you came this morning . . . But if you are too accommodating, she'll keep you here using every means she can . . .

'"I telephoned Bichat in front of her and I was able to inform her that her husband had a good chance of pulling through . . . I exaggerated a little . . . It doesn't really matter, because it's not her husband she feels sorry for but herself . . ."'

The waiter brought the andouillette and chips and half a lobster dressed with mayonnaise. Maigret filled their glasses.

'When you phoned me and I told her I had to leave her for a couple of hours, she said bitterly:

'"Your husband needs you, of course. All men are the same . . ."'

'Then, abruptly changing the subject:'

'"When I'm a widow, my allowance won't be enough to allow me to keep this apartment where I've lived for twenty-five years."'

'She didn't mention the existence of a woman in Lognon's life?'

'She simply said that being a policeman is a vile job, where you mix with all sorts of people, including prostitutes . . .'

'Did you try to find out whether his behaviour had changed recently?'

'She replied:'

'"Ever since I made the stupid mistake of marrying him, he's forever been telling me that he's working on the big case that will bring him glory and force his superiors to promote him to the rank he deserves . . . At first, I believed him and was thrilled for him . . .'

'"In the end, the big case would fizzle out, or someone else would take the credit for it."'

Madame Maigret added, cheerful in a way her husband had rarely seen her:

'I have to confess that the way she looked at me when she said that, it was clear that the person who took all the credit was no other than you . . . She complained recently that he was being asked to do night duty more often than was fair . . . Is that right?'

'He was the one who requested it.'

'He didn't brag about it in front of her . . . Four or five

days ago, he announced that soon there'd be some news and that, this time, the newspapers would be publishing his photo on the front page, whether they liked it or not . . .'

'She didn't try to find out any more?'

'She didn't believe him, and I imagine she laughed at him. Wait! She did add something that struck me. He told her:

'"People aren't always what they seem and, if we could see through walls, there would be some strange surprises . . ."'

They were interrupted by the owner, who came over to greet them and offer them a liqueur. When they were alone again, Madame Maigret asked, a little anxiously:

'Have I been of any help to you? Will that be useful?'

He didn't reply immediately because, as he lit his pipe, he was mulling over an idea that was still half-formed.

'Did you hear?'

'Yes. What you have just told me will probably change the direction of the investigation . . .'

She looked at him, still incredulous, but delighted. That lunch at Chez Manière would be one of her most treasured memories.

3. Marinette's Love Affairs

The rain was beginning to ease up, no longer slanting down furiously and drenching those out and about, and Maigret, looking out of the window, prolonged this exceptionally delightful lunch.

Had Lognon been able to see them, it would have given him yet another reason to vent his bitterness:

'While I lie injured in a hospital bed, others are treating themselves to a romantic lunch at Chez Manière and talking about my poor wife as if she were a shrew or a madwoman . . .'

An idea occurred to Maigret, not necessarily original, or profound:

'It's curious how people's susceptibility generally complicates our lives more than their actual faults or their lies . . .'

This was especially true in his profession. He recalled investigations that had dragged on for several days, if not weeks, because he hadn't dared ask the person in front of him a blunt question, or because they were loath to talk about certain matters.

'Are you returning to your office?'

'I'm going to Avenue Junot first. What about you?'

'You don't think that if I leave her on her own, she'll accuse you of abandoning her with no one to care for her while her husband lies dying as a result of his devotion to the police?'

It was true. Madame Lognon, whose ill-suited first name Solange meant angel of the sun, was capable of complaining to the reporters who would soon be knocking at her door, and goodness knows what they'd end up printing in the newspapers.

'But you can't spend your days and nights at her place until he's better. See if the old spinster with the rosary can help out.'

'Her name's Mademoiselle Papin.'

'For a little money, she's bound to agree to spend a few hours in the apartment. Or you could perhaps hire a nurse . . .'

By the time they left the restaurant the rain had eased up, and they went their separate ways at Place Constantin-Pecqueur. Maigret walked slowly up Avenue Junot and spotted Inspector Chinquier coming out of one building and ringing the bell of the one next door.

That too was a task that was both delicate and disheartening. You disturbed people who were going quietly about their business at home and who were either worried or annoyed by the mere mention of the police.

'May I ask you whether last night . . .'

They were all aware that an attempted murder had taken place in their street. Did they feel they were under suspicion? And is it not sometimes disagreeable to tell a stranger what one was doing the previous night?

Even so, Maigret would have liked to be in Chinquier's shoes, to become better acquainted with the street, its residents, its inner life, which would have helped him understand the context, if not the tragedy itself.

Unfortunately, it was a job that a divisional chief inspector cannot allow himself to do in person, and Maigret was already criticized for being out and about too often instead of managing his men from his office.

There was only one officer left on duty outside Marinette's building. The faint bloodstain on the pavement was still visible. A few passers-by stopped for a moment, without forming a crowd, and the reporters had vanished.

'Nothing new?'

'Nothing, inspector. Things have calmed down . . .'

In the lodge the Saugets were lingering at the table, the night porter at Le Palace still in his unsightly dressing gown, and still unshaven.

'Don't let me disturb you . . . I'm going up to the fourth floor for a minute, but I'd like to ask you one or two questions first . . . I presume Mademoiselle Augier doesn't have a car?'

'She bought herself a scooter two years ago, and sold it two or three months later after a minor accident . . .'

'Where does she usually spend her holidays?'

'Last summer she went to Spain and came back so tanned that I didn't recognize her at first.'

'Alone?'

'With a female friend, so she told me.'

'Did she often have visits from female friends?'

'No. Other than the fiancé I told you about and the inspector who has been coming to see her recently, she lived quite a solitary existence . . .'

'What about Sundays?'

'She would often go away on Saturday evenings, because she worked on Saturday afternoons, and come back on Monday morning. Salons are closed on Monday mornings.'

'So she couldn't have gone very far?'

'What I know is that she went swimming. She would often talk about spending hours in the water . . .'

He climbed up the four flights of stairs, spent a good fifteen minutes opening drawers and cupboards, examining the clothes, underwear and knick-knacks that reveal a person's character and taste.

Although nothing was particularly expensive, everything had been chosen with care. He found a letter, postmarked Grenoble, that he'd missed that morning. In a man's handwriting, the tone affectionate and cheerful, and it was only on reading the closing words that Maigret realized that it came from Marinette's father.

. . . Your sister is pregnant again and her engineer husband is prouder than if he'd built the biggest dam in the world . . . As for your mother, she's still struggling to keep some forty brats under control and comes home in the evening fragrant with the smell of infant wee . . .

A wedding photograph, of her sister's marriage most likely, dating from a few years earlier. Surrounding the couple were the parents, stiff and awkward, as always in these photos, a young man and his wife with a little boy of three in front of them, and finally a woman with lively, shining eyes who must have been Marinette.

He put the photograph in his pocket. A little later, he took a taxi to Quai des Orfèvres, where he went back to his desk, which he'd left at one o'clock in the morning after persevering for hours and hours to try to solve the hold-up case.

He hadn't had the time to remove his overcoat when Janvier knocked on his door.

'I saw the brother, chief. I found him in his office in Rue Le Peletier, where he holds a fairly senior position.'

Maigret showed him the wedding photograph.

'Is that him?'

Without hesitation, Janvier pointed at the father of the little boy.

'Had he heard about what happened last night?'

'No. The newspapers have only just come out. At first, he insisted it must be a mistake, that it wasn't his sister's nature to run away or hide.

'"She's so outspoken that I sometimes reprimand her, because not everyone likes it."'

'You didn't get the feeling that he was keeping something from you?'

Maigret had sat down and fiddled with his pipes before selecting one, which he filled slowly.

'No. He seems like a very decent type. He answered all my questions about the family without hesitation. The father is an English teacher at the Grenoble Lycée and the mother is head of a nursery school. There's another sister in Grenoble, married to an engineer who gives her a baby every year.'

'I know.'

Maigret didn't add that he had learned this from the letter he had found in a drawer.

'After her baccalaureate Marinette decided to live in Paris, where she worked at first as a shorthand typist for a lawyer. Office life didn't suit her, and she trained to become a beautician. Her dream, according to her brother, is to open a beauty salon one day.'

'What about the fiancé?'

'She really was engaged. The young man, whose name is Jean-Claude Ternel, is the son of a Paris industrialist. Marinette introduced him to her brother. There was talk of taking him to Grenoble to meet her parents.'

It is demoralizing, in a criminal case, to be confronted only with normal people, because you wonder why and how they have come to be mixed up in a tragedy.

'Does the brother know that Jean-Claude often used to stay overnight?'

'He didn't dwell on that point, but he gave me to understand that while, as a brother, he couldn't approve, he was modern enough not to criticize his sister.'

'A model family, in other words!' grumbled Maigret.

'I found him very pleasant.'

The apartment in Avenue Junot, which must have reflected Marinette's personality, was pleasant too.

'All the same, I'd like to track her down as soon as possible. Has her brother seen her lately?'

'Not last week but the week before. When she didn't go to the country, she spent Sunday afternoons with her brother and sister-in-law. They live in Vanves, next to the park, which, as François Augier says, is very handy for the children . . .'

'She didn't mention anything to them?'

'She told them, in passing, that she'd met an extraordinary man and that soon she'd have an astonishing story to tell them. Her sister-in-law teased her:

'"A new fiancé?"'

Janvier seemed embarrassed to be reporting such mundane details.

'She swore that no, that once was enough . . .'

'Why did she break up with Jean-Claude?'

'She eventually realized that he was spineless, incapable of effort, and that, deep down, he wasn't so thrilled to be committed. He failed his baccalaureate twice. Then his father sent him to England to stay with a friend, where things went wrong. Finally, he was given an office job in Paris, but he didn't make a success of it.'

'Will you find out what time, either last night or this morning, there was a train for Grenoble?'

That proved fruitless. If she'd taken the first train, Marinette could have been at her parents' house by now. Neither her father, whom they managed to get hold of at school, nor her mother had seen her.

Once again they had to give tactful explanations so as not to worry those good people.

'No, no . . . I'm sure nothing's happened to her . . . Don't worry, Madame Augier . . . It so happens that last night your daughter witnessed a murder . . . No! Not at her place . . . It simply took place on Avenue Junot . . . For reasons that I do

49

not know yet, she has chosen to disappear for a while . . . I thought she might have taken refuge at your house.'

Maigret hung up and turned to Janvier.

'Phew! What on earth could I say to her? . . . Lapointe questioned the girls from the beauty salon this morning and none of them knows where Marinette spent her Sundays . . . She went off without any luggage, without a change of clothes, in the pouring rain. She'd know that in a hotel she'd immediately be spotted.

'Either she's staying with a girlfriend she trusts, or she's gone somewhere she knows well, a discreet place, a guest house in the suburbs, for example . . .

'She's a keen swimmer . . . It is highly unlikely that she could afford to go to the seaside every week . . . There are hundreds of possible spots, by the Seine, the Marne or the Oise . . .

'Go and see this Jean-Claude and try to find out where they used to go.'

Moers, in the adjacent office, was waiting for his turn, carrying a little cardboard box containing the bullets and the three cartridges.

'The expert agrees, chief. It is definitely a 7.63 calibre and the gun used is almost certainly a Mauser.'

'Fingerprints?'

'I wonder what you'll think. They found Inspector Lognon's all over the living room, including on the wireless knobs . . .'

'Not on those of the television?'

'No. In the kitchen, he opened the refrigerator and a tin of ground coffee . . . His prints were also found on the electric coffee-maker . . . Why are you smiling? Am I saying something stupid?'

'No. Go on.'

'Lognon used the glass and the cup. As for the bottle of brandy, it has both Lognon and the young woman's prints on it.'

'What about the bedroom?'

'No trace of Lognon. Not one of his hairs on the pillow but a woman's hair. Not the slightest trace of mud either, even though, from what I was told, Lognon arrived at Avenue Junot in the pouring rain.'

With Moers and his team, no detail was neglected.

'He seems to have stayed sitting in the armchair in front of one of the French windows. I suppose that's when he turned the radio on. At another moment, he opened that window, leaving a perfect set of prints on the handle, and I picked up one of his cigarette ends from the balcony. You're still smiling . . .'

'Because that confirms the hunch I had earlier while listening to my wife talk . . .'

Did not everything suggest that Hard-Done-By, reduced to slavery by his wife, had finally allowed himself a love affair, and that he consoled himself at Avenue Junot for the dismal hours spent in the apartment in Place Constantin-Pecqueur?

'I'm smiling, Moers my friend, at the idea that his colleagues suddenly think he's a Don Juan. I'd swear, you see, that there was nothing going on between them, and I'm almost sad for him that there wasn't.

'He spent his evenings in the front room, the living

room, generally by the window, and young Mademoiselle Marinette trusted him sufficiently to go to bed, despite his presence . . .

'You didn't find anything else?'

'A little sand, in the young woman's shoes, flat shoes that she must have worn in the countryside. It's river sand. We have hundreds of different samples up there, but it will take hours, and a lot of luck, to identify where that sand comes from.'

'Keep me posted . . . Is anyone else waiting for me next door?'

'An inspector from the eighteenth.'

'With a little brown moustache?'

'Yes.'

'That's Chinquier. Tell him to come in as you go past.'

It was starting to rain again, a fine drizzle, a sort of fog that softened the light. The clouds in the sky were barely moving and gradually turning into a dense grey canopy.

'Well, Chinquier?'

'I haven't finished with the street and my men are still making door-to-door inquiries. Luckily there are only forty or so numbers on each side. That's still some two hundred people to be questioned.'

'What interests me most of all are the buildings opposite.'

'If you'll allow me, sir, I'll come to that in a minute, because I think I know what you're driving at. I began with the residents of the building poor Lognon came out of. On the ground floor, there's only an elderly couple, the

Guèbres, who have been in Mexico for a month, visiting their married daughter who lives there . . .'

From his pocket he'd produced an old notebook, several pages of which were covered with names and sketches. With him too, you had to take things slowly to avoid upsetting him.

'The other floors all have two apartments. On the first floor is a widow, Madame Faisant, who's a sales assistant in a fashion house, and a couple of independent means, the Laniers, who rushed over to the window immediately after the shooting. They saw the car drive off, but they weren't able to make out the number plate.'

His eyes half closed, Maigret listened vaguely to the inspector's meticulous report, as if to a hum, occasionally drawing on his pipe.

He began to pay attention when he heard the name of a certain Maclet, who occupied the second floor of the building next door. According to Chinquier, he was a cantankerous old man who had shut himself away once and for all, content to watch the world from his window with a cynical expression.

'He's crippled with rheumatism and drags himself around with two sticks, in a filthy apartment where no cleaning woman is allowed to cross the threshold. Each day, he places a note on his doormat to order food, which the concierge leaves outside his door.

'He doesn't have a wireless, doesn't read the newspapers. The concierge claims he's rich, even though he lives almost like a pauper. He has a married daughter, who's tried several times to have him put away . . .'

'Is he really mad?'

'You'll see. I had a terrible job getting him to open his door to me and I had to threaten to come back with a locksmith. When he finally made up his mind, he looked me up and down for ages, sighing:

'"You're a bit young for this job, aren't you?"'

'I replied that I was thirty-five and he repeated two or three times:

'"A boy! . . . A boy! . . . What does a person know at thirty-five? How much is a person capable of understanding?"'

'Did he tell you anything new?'

'He spoke to me mainly about the Dutchman opposite . . . It's the building we saw this morning from the balcony, the little private mansion with the second floor glazed like an artist's studio . . .

'That house was built fifteen years ago by a certain Norris Jonker, who is now sixty-four and whose wife, a beauty by all accounts, is much younger than him . . .'

Once again, Maigret wished he could have carried out these door-to-door inquiries himself. He would like to have met this rheumatic old misanthrope who had withdrawn from the world in the middle of Paris, in the middle of Montmartre, and spent his time spying on the people across the road.

'All of a sudden he became talkative. Since he has a habit of jumping from one idea to another and slipping commentaries into his speech, I'm worried I might leave something out . . .

'I saw the Dutchman later, and it would be best if I told

you about him straight away . . . He's a charming, elegant and cultured man who belongs to a very well-known and very wealthy family in Holland . . . His father was the head of the Jonker, Haag & Company Bank in Amsterdam . . . He himself has never been interested in finance and he spent years travelling the world.

'When he realized that the only place where he was happy was Paris, he had this mansion built in Avenue Junot, while his brother Hans has taken over the running of the bank since their father's death.

'Norris Jonker is content to receive the dividends and convert them into paintings—'

'Paintings?' echoed Maigret.

'He's said to own one of the most beautiful art collections in Paris—'

'Just a moment! . . . You rang the bell . . . Who opened the door?'

'A very fair-haired, rosy-cheeked manservant, quite young . . .'

'Did you say you were from the police?'

'Yes. He didn't seem surprised and he showed me into the entrance hall where he offered me a seat . . . I don't know anything about art, but I deciphered the signatures of painters even I'd heard of: Gauguin, Cézanne, Renoir . . . Lots of nude women . . .'

'Did you wait for long?'

'About ten minutes . . . The double door between the hall and the drawing room was open and I saw a young woman with black hair walk past, still in her bathrobe, at three o'clock in the afternoon . . . I could be wrong, but I

had the impression that she had come to inspect me . . .
A few minutes later, the manservant invited me to cross
the drawing room and I was shown into a study lined with
books from floor to ceiling . . .

'I was greeted by Norris Jonker, dressed in flannel trousers, an open-necked silk shirt and a black velvet jacket . . .
His hair is very white, his complexion almost as rosy as
that of his servant . . .

'There was a tray with a decanter and glasses on the
desk.

'"Have a seat . . . How can I help . . . ?" he asked without
the trace of an accent.'

It was clear that Inspector Chinquier had been over-
whelmed by the opulence and the paintings as much as
by the Dutchman's distinguished air.

'I confess I didn't know where to begin . . . I asked him
whether he'd heard the shots and he replied that no, his
bedroom was on the other side of the house from Avenue
Junot, and that you couldn't hear much through the thick
walls.

'"I hate noise," he told me before offering me a glass of
a liqueur that was new to me, a very strong liqueur, with
an aftertaste of orange . . .

'"But you must be aware of what happened last night
across the street from your house?"

'"Carl spoke to me about it when he brought me my
breakfast, at around ten. He's my manservant, the son of
one of our farmers. He told me that Avenue Junot was in
turmoil because a police officer had been attacked by
gangsters."'

'How did he sound?' asked Maigret, fiddling with his pipe.

'Calm, smiling, unexpectedly polite for a man who has been disturbed without warning.'

'"If you wish to question Carl, I will gladly put him at your disposal, but he also sleeps on the garden side of the house and he stated that he hadn't heard anything either."'

'"Are you married, Monsieur Jonker?"'

'"I most certainly am. My wife was shocked to hear what had happened a few metres from our home."'

At this point in his report, Chinquier displayed a slight awkwardness.

'I don't know if I did the right thing, chief. I would have liked to ask him a lot of other questions. I didn't dare, telling myself that ultimately, it was more urgent to update you . . .'

'So let's go back to the elderly invalid.'

'Exactly. It's because of him that I'd have liked to talk to the Dutchman about certain things. One of the first things Maclet said, in fact, was:

'"What would you do, inspector, if you were married to one of the most beautiful women in Paris? . . . Ha! Ha! You're not answering . . . And you're a long way off sixty-four or sixty-five . . . Right! Let's put it another way . . . What does a man of that age do who has a magnificent creature available to him day and night?

'"Well! The gentleman opposite must have very particular ideas on the subject . . . I sleep little . . . I'm not interested in politics or the disasters that the radio and the newspapers talk about . . .

'"I entertain myself by thinking . . . You understand? . . . I look out of the window and I think . . . Few people realize how amusing it is to think . . .

'"For example, about that Dutchman and his wife . . . They don't go out much – once or twice a week, her in an evening gown, him in a dinner-jacket, and they rarely come home after one o'clock in the morning, which means that they are content to have dinner with friends or go to the theatre . . .

'"They themselves never have dinner parties . . . Nor do they have guests for luncheon . . . And what's more, they rarely eat before three o'clock in the afternoon . . .

'"You see . . . A person entertains himself as best he can . . . He watches . . . He guesses . . . He puts two and two together . . .

'"So when a couple of times a week he sees a pretty girl ring the doorbell, at around eight o'clock in the evening, and not leave until very late at night, if not at dawn . . ."'

Maigret most definitely regretted not having questioned that eccentric old man.

'"And that's not all, Mister police inspector . . . Admit that my ramblings are beginning to interest you . . . Especially if I tell you that it is never the same young lady . . .

'"They usually arrive by taxi, sometimes on foot . . . From my window, I see them looking at the numbers on the buildings, which means something too, don't you agree?

'"It means they've been asked to come to a particular address . . .

'"You know I haven't always been an old, sick animal shut away in his lair, and I know a thing or two about women . . .

'"And you can also recognize those who live on the edge, so to speak – cabaret dancers, theatre or film extras who won't say no to the chance to earn a bit of cash . . ."'

Maigret sprang to his feet.

'I say, Chinquier, do you get it?'

'Get what?'

'How it all started for Lognon. At night, he often walked down Avenue Junot, where he knew most of the residents . . . If, on several occasions, he saw the women you describe going into the Dutchman's house . . .'

'I thought of that too. But there's no law against a man, even of a certain age, enjoying variety.'

True, that wasn't a sufficient reason for Hard-Done-By to seek and find a way of staking out a private residence.

'There must be an explanation.'

'What?'

'That he was waiting for one of these visitors to leave. It's even possible that he came across a prostitute he'd had dealings with before . . .'

'I see . . . Even so, everyone is free to . . .'

'It depends what went on in the house, or on what the woman saw there . . . What else did this charming old man tell you?'

Because Maigret felt increasingly drawn to the strange fellow at his window.

'I asked him all the questions that occurred to me and wrote down all his replies.'

Chinquier consulted his black notebook again.

'Question: Did these women not come for the servant?

'Reply: First of all, the manservant is in love with the dairymaid at the bottom of the street, a plump little thing who's always bursting out laughing . . . She comes and waits for him several nights a week . . . She stays in the shadows, about ten metres from the house, I could show you the exact spot, and he soon appears . . .

'Question: At around what time?

'Reply: At around ten . . . I suppose he waits at table, and the Jonkers tend to eat late . . . The pair go for a stroll, arm in arm, stop to kiss and, before parting, cling to each other for a good while in the recess you see to the right . . .

'Question: He doesn't walk her home?

'Reply: No. She walks down the street alone, happy, skipping . . . She sometimes looks as if she's about to start dancing . . . There's another reason why it is impossible that the women I told you about would be seeing the manservant . . . On several occasions they have rung at the door in his absence . . .

'Question: Who opened the door?

'Reply: Precisely! . . . Here's another very funny peculiarity . . . Sometimes it's the Dutchman, and sometimes his wife . . .

'Question: Do they have a car?

'Reply: Yes. A big American car.

'Question: A driver?

'Reply: Carl puts on a chauffeur's livery and drives.

'Question: Are there other live-in servants?

'Reply: A cook and two maids . . . The maids often don't stay long . . .

'Question: Do they receive many visitors, apart from the ladies in question?

'Reply: A few . . . The one who drops by most often, in the afternoons, is a man of around forty, American-looking, who drives a yellow sports car . . .

'Question: Does he stay long?

'Reply: An hour or two . . .

'Question: He never comes in the evening, or at night?

'Reply: I've seen him in the evening twice, around a month ago, at around ten o'clock, in the company of a young woman. He simply went in and came straight out, leaving his companion in the house.

'Question: Was it the same woman both times?

'Reply: No.'

Maigret imagined the sardonic, almost sensual smile of the old man who revealed these small mysteries.

'Reply: There's also a man who's bald, even though he's still young, who arrives by taxi, after dark, and who leaves carrying packages.

'Question: What kind of packages?

'Reply: They could be paintings. They could also be just about anything . . .

'"That's more or less everything I know, inspector . . . I haven't talked so much for years, and I hope I don't have to do so again for a long time . . . I warn you, there's no point summoning me to a police station or to an investigating magistrate's chambers . . .

'"And above all, don't count on me to testify in court, if this case gets that far . . .

'"We've had a chat . . . I've told you my little ideas. Now they're yours and I refuse to put myself out for any reason whatsoever . . ."'

Immediately afterwards, Chinquier was to prove that the local inspectors knew their job.

'Later, as I was coming out of the Dutchman's house, I wondered whether the fellow opposite had been making fun of me. I thought that, if I could check one of the things he'd told me, that would make the rest credible.

'So I stopped by the dairy. I waited outside until the girl was alone in the shop. She was indeed the plump little thing the old fellow had described, a girl recently arrived from the country and who was still thrilled to find herself in Paris . . .

'I went in and asked her:

'"Do you know a certain Carl?"

'She blushed, and turned anxiously towards an open door, whispering:

'"Who are you? What's it got to do with you?"

'"A simple piece of information. I'm from the police."

'"What's he done?"

'"Nothing. It's a routine check. Are you engaged?"

'"We may get married one day, but he hasn't asked me yet . . ."

'"Do you see him several evenings a week?"

'"Whenever I can . . ."

'"Do you wait for him a few metres from the house on Avenue Junot?"

'"Who told you?"

'Then a large woman appeared from the backroom, and she had the presence of mind to say loudly:

'"No, monsieur, we don't have any Gorgonzola left, but we do have some Roquefort . . . They're very similar . . ."'

Maigret smiled.

'Did you buy some Roquefort?'

'I said that my wife only liked Gorgonzola . . . That's all, chief . . . I don't know what my colleagues will bring me this evening . . . Any news of poor old Lognon?'

'I had one of my men call the hospital earlier. The doctors still won't comment, and he hasn't regained consciousness. It's feared that the second bullet, which hit him below the shoulder, might have damaged the top of his right lung, but it's impossible to X-ray him in his present condition.'

'I wonder what he found out to get himself shot . . . You'll be as surprised as me when you've seen the Dutchman . . . I can't imagine that a man like him—'

'There is one thing I'd like you to do, Chinquier . . . When your men are back, and especially when the night shift come on duty, have them all deal with the women . . . Some of them, you said, arrived at Avenue Junot on foot, so they may be local . . .

'Have them go over the nightclubs with a fine-tooth comb . . . From your invalid's descriptions, I don't think we need to look on the streets . . . if you get my drift?

'Sooner or later we'll come across one who's been to Avenue Junot . . .'

It would probably have been more useful to find Marinette Augier. Would Moers and the laboratory team, with their sand samples, give him a lead at last?

4. The Visit to the Dutchman

'Hello! This is the Dutch embassy . . .'

The young, cheerful voice with a slight accent made him think of the windmills on certain cocoa tins.

'I'd like to speak to the first secretary, mademoiselle.'

'Who's calling?'

'Detective Chief Inspector Maigret, of the Police Judiciaire.'

'One moment. I'll see if Mr Goudekamp is in his office.'

The voice was back after a little while.

'Mr Goudekamp is in a meeting, but I'll put you through to the second secretary, Mr de Vries . . . Please hold the line . . .'

A man's voice this time, less cheerful, naturally, and with a stronger accent.

'Hubert de Vries speaking, Second Secretary of the Dutch embassy.'

'Detective Chief Inspector Maigret, head of the Crime Squad.'

'How can I help you?'

De Vries, on the other end of the line, was probably starchy and suspicious, young most likely, because he was still only second secretary, fair-haired perhaps, slightly overdressed, in the manner of people from northern Europe.

'I'd like some information about one of your citizens who has lived in Paris for a long time and whose name is probably very familiar to you . . .'

'Where are you at the moment, Monsieur Maigret?'

'In my office at Quai des Orfèvres.'

'Please don't be offended if I call you back shortly.'

Five minutes went by before the phone rang.

'My apologies, Monsieur Maigret, but all sorts of people telephone us and some claim to be someone they are not. You wanted to talk to me about a Dutch subject who lives in Paris?'

'About Norris Jonker . . .'

Why did Maigret have the feeling that the invisible second secretary was suddenly on his guard?

'Yes . . .'

'Do you know him?'

'Jonker is a very common name in Holland, rather like Durand in France. Norris isn't an unusual first name either.'

'This Norris Jonker is related to the Amsterdam banking family.'

'The Jonker, Haag & Company Bank is one of the longest established in the country. Old Kees Jonker died around fifteen years ago and his son Hans, unless I'm mistaken, is at the helm of the firm.'

'What about Norris Jonker?'

'I don't know him personally.'

'But you are aware of his existence?'

'Definitely. I think he's a member of the Saint-Cloud golf club, where our paths may inadvertently have crossed . . .'

'Is he married?'

'To an Englishwoman, so I've been told. May I ask you now, Monsieur Maigret, why you are interested in Norris Jonker?'

'Only very indirectly.'

'Have you seen him?'

'Not yet.'

'Do you not think it would be simpler to obtain the information you require from the man himself? I should be able to give you his address.'

'I know it.'

'Norris Jonker has little to do with the embassy. He belongs to a family that is both prominent and respectable, and I have every reason to believe that he himself is an upstanding man. He is reputed above all for his art collection.'

'You don't have any information about his wife either?'

'I would feel more comfortable replying if I knew the reason for your questions. Madame Jonker, from what I've heard, is from the south of France and was married to an Englishman, Herbert Muir from Manchester, a ball-bearings manufacturer.'

'They don't have any children?'

'Not to my knowledge.'

Maigret understood that he would not glean any more information, so he then called another number, that of an auctioneer he'd been in touch with on several occasions and who was often called upon as an expert witness in court.

'Monsieur Manessi? Maigret here . . .'

'Just a moment while I close the door ... Right! What can I do for you ... Are you interested in art these days?'

'I'm not sure. Do you know a Dutchman by the name of Norris Jonker?'

'The one who lives in Avenue Junot? Not only do I know him, but I've done valuations for him. He owns one of the finest collections of late nineteenth-century and early twentieth-century paintings.'

'That suggests he's very wealthy?'

'His father was a banker and an art lover. Norris Jonker was brought up surrounded by Van Goghs, Pissarros, Manets and Renoirs. It's not surprising that he had no interest in the bank. He inherited a good share of the paintings, and the dividends that the bank, managed by his brother, bring him, give him the means to expand his collection ...'

'Have you met him in person?'

'Yes. Have you?'

'Not yet.'

'He's more like an English gentleman than a Dutchman. If I remember correctly, after studying at Oxford he lived in England for many years, and I've heard that he ended the last war as a colonel in the British army.'

'What about his wife?'

'A stunning creature who was married very young to an Englishman from Manchester—'

'Ball-bearings, I know ...'

'I wonder why you're interested in Jonker. I hope he hasn't been victim of a painting theft?'

'No.'

Now it was Maigret's turn to be evasive.

'Do they go out much?'

'Not that I'm aware of.'

'Does Jonker socialize with other art lovers?'

'He keeps his eye on the auctions, naturally, and he knows when an important painting is being sold at Drouot, Galliera, Sotheby's or in New York . . .'

'Does he travel?'

'You're asking me too much. He has travelled extensively, but I don't know if he still does. Collectors don't necessarily bother to attend in person to buy a painting at a public auction. On the contrary, the major buyers usually send a representative—'

'In short, he's a man you can trust?'

'Sure as can be.'

'Thank you.'

That did not make things any easier, and Maigret rose without enthusiasm to fetch his overcoat and hat from the cupboard.

The better known important and respectable people are, the more delicate it is to ring at their door to question them, and it is not rare for them to complain to those at the top, which bodes ill for the police officer.

Maigret was loath to take one of his inspectors with him and decided to go to Avenue Junot alone, so as to make his visit less official.

Half an hour later, a taxi dropped him off in front of the private residence, and he handed his card to Carl, the manservant in a white jacket. He was shown into the entrance hall, like Inspector Chinquier before him, but, perhaps because of his rank, he was kept waiting only five minutes instead of ten.

'If you would follow me . . .'

Carl preceded him across the drawing room, where Maigret did not have the opportunity of meeting the beautiful Madame Jonker, and opened the door to the study. The Dutchman had not changed his clothes, or, so it appeared, his position. Sitting at an Empire-style desk, he was studying some etchings with the help of a giant illuminated magnifying glass.

He rose at once, and Maigret was able to note that the description he'd been given was accurate. With his grey flannel trousers, soft silk shirt and black velvet jacket, he was the quintessential English gentleman at home. He also had the stiff upper lip. Neither surprised nor perturbed, he said:

'Monsieur Maigret?'

He indicated a leather armchair, on the other side of the desk, and sat down again.

'I am very flattered, believe me, to meet a man of your renown . . .'

He spoke slowly, as if, after so many years, he was still thinking in Dutch and had to translate every word.

'I am a little surprised to receive a second visit from the police . . .'

He waited, gazing at his plump, manicured hands. He wasn't fat but had what used to be called an imposing bearing and could have been a model for a drawing in *La Vie Parisienne* circa 1900.

His face was a little flabby, his blue eyes visible behind frameless glasses with thin gold sides.

Maigret began, not without a certain embarrassment:

'Inspector Chinquier did indeed inform me of his visit. He's a neighbourhood inspector and does not work directly for our department . . .'

'Should I understand that you need to verify his report?'

'Not exactly. But perhaps he didn't ask all the questions he should have asked.'

The Dutchman, who was toying with the magnifying glass, looked directly at Maigret, and there was a mixture of mischief and a hint of innocence in his blue eyes.

'Listen to me, Monsieur Maigret. I am sixty-four years old and I have lived in many countries. I have been settled for a long time in France, where I am so happy that I have built my home here.

'I have no criminal record and I have never set foot in a courtroom or a police station.

'Apparently some shots were fired in the street last night, opposite my home. As I told the inspector, neither I nor my wife heard anything, because our bedrooms are on the other side of the house.

'Tell me, what would you think if you were in my shoes and I in yours?'

'I would certainly view these visits as disagreeable, because it is never pleasing to have people you don't know come into your home . . .'

'I'm sorry! I'm sorry! I am not complaining at having you sitting here, on the contrary, it is an opportunity to meet someone about whom I have heard a great deal. I look at things, as you know, from a different perspective.

'Your inspector asked me some rather indiscreet questions but not too many, ultimately, given his job. I don't know what you plan to ask, but I am surprised that such a high-ranking official should take the trouble to come in person.'

'If I were to reply that it is out of deference—'

'I would be flattered while unwilling to believe you. And perhaps it would be wiser of me to find out whether your presence here is lawful.'

'I would have no objection, Monsieur Jonker, and you are free to telephone your lawyer. Let me add that I have come without a warrant and it is your right to ask me to leave. All the same, it is clear that a lack of cooperation on your part would likely be interpreted as hostility, or even the wish to hide something . . .'

The Dutchman smiled in his armchair and reached for a box of cigars.

'You smoke, I think?'

'Only a pipe.'

'Feel free.'

He himself selected a cigar, holding it to his ear and rustling it, then he clipped one end with a gold cigar-cutter and slowly lit it, with an almost ritual gesture.

'One more question,' he said between two puffs of pretty blue smoke. 'Am I to understand that I am the only person in Avenue Junot to have the honour of your visit, or is this case so important that you will be going from house to house in person to question the residents?'

Maigret too was choosing his words carefully:

'You are not the first person in the street that I am questioning. My inspectors are going from house to house, as you say, but as far as you are concerned, I believed it was my duty to take the trouble . . .'

Jonker appeared to be thanking him with a nod, but he didn't believe a word.

'I will try and answer you, so long as you do not intrude into my private life.'

Maigret was about to open his mouth when the telephone rang.

'May I?'

Jonker picked up the receiver and replied in English briefly, frowning. Maigret's schoolboy English was not that good and had not been much use in London, and even less during his two trips to the United States, although people had taken great pains to try to understand him.

But at least he knew that the Dutchman resented not being free, and that, in answer to a question asked by the invisible caller, he said:

'From the same firm, yes . . . I'll call you back later . . .'

Presumably that meant that he was busy with someone from the same profession as the inspector who'd been there earlier?

'Excuse me . . . I am all yours . . .'

He settled into a comfortable pose, reclining slightly in his chair, his elbows on the arm-rests, sometimes glancing at the white ash on his cigar, which was gradually growing longer.

'You asked me, Monsieur Jonker, what I would do in

your shoes. I would like to ask you what you would do in mine. When a crime is committed, in this district or another, there are always neighbours who remember odd details they hadn't noticed before or which they hadn't thought were of any importance.'

'I believe you call that gossip, don't you?'

'If you like. The fact is that it is our duty to check because, although many of these people are fantasists, some give us valuable leads.'

'So let us hear this gossip.'

But Maigret had no intention of getting straight to the point. He still couldn't make up his mind whether Jonker was a mischievous but decent man or whether, on the contrary, he was someone very clever who remained on his guard while acting the innocent.

'You are a married man, Monsieur Jonker.'

'Does that surprise you?'

'No. I have been told that Madame Jonker is a very beautiful woman.'

'I am asking you again: does that surprise you? Admittedly, I am a man of a certain age, many would say an old man, perhaps adding that I am fairly well preserved.

'Whereas my wife is only thirty-four, which makes an age difference of exactly thirty years. Do you think we are the only ones in this situation, in Paris or elsewhere? Is it so shocking?'

'Is Madame Jonker French?'

'I can see you have done your research. She was born in Nice, yes, but I met her in London.'

'Was she married previously?'

73

Jonker displayed some impatience, which could have been that of a gentleman outraged at having his private life raked over and above all at being asked about his wife.

'She was Mrs Muir before being Madame Jonker,' he snapped.

He added, after staring at his cigar for a while:

'You should know too, since you insist on raising the subject, that she didn't marry me for my money, because she was already what is called independently wealthy.'

'You go out fairly little for a man of your situation, Monsieur Jonker.'

'Is that a criticism? You know, I spent most of my life going out, either here, in London, in the USA, India, Australia or elsewhere. When you are my age—'

'I'm not so far off . . .'

'When you are my age, I was saying, you will probably prefer being at home to society gatherings, clubs and nightclubs.'

'I understand you all the better because you must be very much in love with Madame Jonker . . .'

This time the former British colonel tensed, and his only reply was a jerk of his head, which made the ash fall from his cigar.

The delicate moment, which Maigret had put off as long as possible, was approaching, and he gave himself a little more time by lighting his pipe, which had gone out.

'You used the word "gossip" and I am prepared to believe, if you say it is so, that certain intelligence that we have received belongs in that category . . .'

Was not the Dutchman's hand trembling slightly? All

the same, he reached for the crystal decanter and poured himself a glass.

'Do you like Curaçao?'

'No thank you.'

'Do you prefer whisky?'

Without waiting for the reply, he pressed a bell. Carl appeared at once.

'Scotch, please . . . Still or sparkling water?'

'Sparkling.'

During this interval they were silent, and Maigret glanced at the bookshelves lining the walls. They contained mainly art books, not only on painting but on the architecture and sculpture of Antiquity, and there were also bound catalogues from the major auctions of the past forty years.

'Thank you, Carl. Have you informed madame that I am busy?'

Out of politeness, he had chosen to speak to his manservant in French.

'Is she still upstairs?'

'Yes, monsieur . . .'

'And now, Monsieur Maigret, I drink to your health and am ready to hear this gossip you mentioned . . .'

'I don't know what it is like in Holland, but in Paris a lot of people, especially the elderly, even more in Montmartre than anywhere else, spend a deal of their time at their window . . . One such person told us that frequently, often two or three times a week, young women ring at your door in the evening and are let into the house . . .'

The Dutchman's ears had suddenly turned red and, without answering, he puffed on his cigar.

'I might have thought that these women were friends of Madame Jonker's if they did not come from a particular milieu, which would be insulting to her . . .'

Rarely had he chosen his words with such care. Rarely too had he felt so uncomfortable.

'Do you deny that these visits took place?'

'If you have troubled yourself to come here, Monsieur Maigret, it is because you are certain of your facts. Admit it! Admit that if I were to have the unfortunate idea of contradicting you, you would put me in front of one or several witnesses . . .'

'You haven't answered my question.'

'What have you been told about these young women?'

'I asked you a question, and you have replied with another.'

'I am in my own home, aren't I? If I were in your office, we would both be in a different position.'

Maigret preferred to give in.

'Let us suppose that these persons belong to the category of what is called loose women. They do not simply come in and leave but spend part of the night, if not the whole night, in the house . . .'

'That is correct.'

He did not look away, on the contrary, but the blue of his eyes had clouded to grey.

To pluck up the courage to continue, Maigret had to think of Lognon in his hospital bed and of the stranger who had viciously aimed one of the deadliest weapons at his stomach.

Jonker wasn't helping him. He sat there as impassive as a poker player.

'If I am mistaken, please stop me. At first, I thought that these young ladies were coming to see your manservant; then I learned that he has a girlfriend and that he is sometimes outside with her at the time of the visits I mentioned.

'May I ask you where your servant's bedroom is?'

'On the second floor, near the studio.'

'Do the maids and the cook sleep on the second floor as well?'

'No. There is an annexe in the garden where the three women sleep.'

'Do you often happen to open the door to these nocturnal female visitors?'

He answered neither yes nor no but continued to stare into Maigret's eyes.

'I'm sorry to add that, according to my source, Madame Jonker showed them into the house on several occasions . . .'

'We are kept under close watch, aren't we? You people are even worse than the old women in our little Dutch villages. Would you tell me now what connection you have established between these visits, alleged or real, and the shots fired in the street?

'Because I refuse to accept that I am being targeted personally and that, for a reason that escapes me, someone is trying to make me *persona non grata* . . .'

'That is out of the question and I'll try to put all my cards on the table. The way last night's tragedy unfolded, the weapon used and some other details which I'm not at liberty to reveal, give me reason to believe that the marksman was a professional.'

77

'And you think I am in contact with these people?'

'I'm going to make a completely gratuitous supposition. You are considered to be a very wealthy man, Monsieur Jonker. This house contains more artworks than a lot of provincial museums and their value is probably priceless . . .'

'Does the building have an alarm system?'

'No. The real professionals, as you call them, make a mockery of the most sophisticated systems, as was proved recently in your very own country. I prefer to be properly insured . . .'

'Have you ever been the victim of an attempted break-in?'

'Not to my knowledge.'

'Can you vouch for your household staff?'

'Carl and the cook, who have been with me for over twenty years, yes. I don't know the maids so well, but my wife didn't hire them without requesting reliable references. You still haven't explained the connection between what you call my female visitors and . . .'

'I'm leading up to it . . .'

So far, Maigret hadn't done too badly, and he rewarded himself with a sip of whisky.

'Supposing a gang of art thieves, of which there are a number in this world, were planning to rob you . . . Supposing a local police inspector got wind of it but too vaguely to take direct action . . . Supposing that, last night, as on previous nights, that inspector had been stationed opposite your house so as to catch the thieves red-handed . . .'

'That would have been imprudent of him, don't you think?'

78

'In our profession, Monsieur Jonker, we are often obliged to be imprudent . . .'

'I'm sorry . . .'

'Although the gangs that specialize in art thefts sometimes hire a hit-man, they are generally made up of intelligent, cultured people who do not act without doing their homework . . . Since you can vouch for your staff, all I can think of is that one of these young ladies . . .'

Did Jonker believe Maigret's line of reasoning or did he smell a rat? It was impossible to tell.

'The young women who work in nightclubs tend to hobnob with the crime world . . .'

'Have you come to ask me for a list – names, addresses and telephone numbers – of the girls who have come here?'

His irony was becoming acerbic.

'That would perhaps be useful, but most of all I would like to know what they came to do in your house.'

Whew! He was almost there. Jonker, stock-still, his cigar between his fingers, continued to stare straight at him without batting an eyelid.

'Right!' he said at length, rising to his feet.

And, after putting his cigar end down in a blue ashtray, he took a few steps forward.

'I told you at the beginning of this interview that I would answer all your questions, so long as they didn't concern my private life. You very skilfully – and I congratulate you – put this private life on the table by linking it to the events of last night.'

He stopped in front of Maigret, who had also got to his feet.

'You have been a member of the police for a long time, I think?'

'Twenty-eight years.'

'I presume you haven't only investigated the underworld. Is this the first time you have seen a man of my age and in my situation give in to certain instincts and do you consider that reprehensible?

'Paris is not considered a puritanical city, Monsieur Maigret. In my country, people would point at me and my family would perhaps disown me.

'A lot of foreigners who live here or on the Riviera have chosen France purely for the freedom enjoyed in these things . . .'

'May I ask whether Madame Jonker . . .'

'Madame Jonker is not a puritan and knows about life. She is not unaware that some men of my age need change to stimulate them . . . You have forced me to speak of very private things and I hope you are satisfied now . . .'

From the way he was looking at the door, he appeared to consider the interview over.

Maigret, however, ploughed on, softly, in an undertone.

'Earlier you mentioned names, addresses and telephone numbers . . .'

'I hope you aren't asking me for them? These individuals may not be leading exemplary lives, but they are not accountable to the police, and it would be improper of me to put them in an awkward situation . . .'

'You told me that you went out seldom and that you don't go to nightclubs. So how did you meet your female visitors?'

Further silence. Further hesitation.

'Do you not know how these things work?' he sighed at last.

'There are pimps and madams, but their activity constitutes an offence.'

'And does their clients' activity constitute an offence too?'

'They could possibly be accused of complicity, but, generally . . .'

'Generally, the clients are left in peace, is that not so? In that case, Monsieur Maigret, I don't think I have anything more to say to you.'

'But I do have one more request for you.'

'Is it really a request? Is that not a euphemism?'

It was now almost open war between the two men.

'Well, if you were to refuse, I might have to resort to legal means.'

'So what is this request . . .'

'I would like a tour of your house.'

'Isn't the word "to search"?'

'You are forgetting that, until now, I have been working from the hypothesis that you were a potential victim . . .'

'And you wish to protect me?'

'Maybe.'

'Come, then . . .'

There was no longer any question of offering Maigret a cigar or pouring him a drink. Jonker's manner had suddenly become very superior, if not lordly.

'You have seen the room where I spend most of my day. Do I have to open the drawers?'

'No.'

'For your information, the one on the right contains an automatic pistol, a Lüger, which I brought back from the war.'

He took it out, adding:

'It is loaded . . . I have another one, a Browning, in my bedroom, also loaded. I'll show it to you later . . .

'This is the drawing room . . . I know you're not here to admire the paintings, but I do advise you have a look at this Gauguin, which is considered one of his finest works and which I'll bequeath to the Amsterdam Museum . . .

'This way . . . Do you know anything about carpets? . . . Never mind . . . Here we are in the dining room, and the painting to the left of the chimney breast is Cézanne's last work . . .

'This door leads into a little room which I designed to be intimate, very feminine, and is my wife's small parlour . . .

'. . . The scullery . . . Carl busy cleaning the silver-ware . . . It is seventeenth-century English silverware whose only drawback is that it is unwieldy . . .

'The kitchen is in the basement . . . The cook too . . . Do you really want to go down?'

Whether intentional or not, there was something insulting in his easy manner.

'Now let us go upstairs . . . The staircase comes from an old castle near Utrecht . . . To the left, my apartment . . .'

He opened the doors like an estate agent showing a prospective buyer around a house.

'Another study, you see, like on the ground floor . . . I love books and they are very useful to me . . . These files on the left contain the history of several thousand paintings, with the list of their successive owners and the price they sold for at each auction . . .

'My bedroom . . . In the bedside-table drawer, the automatic I mentioned . . . A common 6.5 that wouldn't be much use if I were threatened . . .'

Everywhere, even on the walls of the staircase, the paintings were almost touching each other, and the best ones were not in the drawing room but in the Dutchman's bedroom, a very understated room with English furniture and deep leather armchairs.

'My bathroom . . . Now let us go over to the other side, but allow me to check that my wife isn't in her room . . .'

He knocked, opened the door a fraction, and took a few steps into the room.

'You may follow me . . . Her boudoir, for which I found these two Fragonards . . . The wing chairs belonged to Madame de Pompadour . . . If you were here as an art lover, Monsieur Maigret, and not as a detective, I would be delighted to talk to you about each piece . . . The bedroom . . .'

All draped in crushed strawberry satin.

'The bathroom . . .'

Maigret did not go in but glimpsed a bath tub that was more like a black marble pool with several steps down.

'Let us go up to the next floor . . . You are entitled to see everything, isn't that so?'

He opened another door.

'Carl's bedroom . . . And, beyond, the bathroom . . . You will note that he has a television . . . He prefers black and white images to art masterpieces . . .'

He knocked at the door opposite, a heavy, ornately carved door, which must have come from some castle too.

'May I, darling? . . . I am showing Monsieur Maigret around the house. He is head of the Crime Squad . . . That is correct, isn't it, detective chief inspector?'

Maigret had just received a shock. In the middle of the glazed studio, standing at an easel, was a white shape that reminded him of the words Lognon had said: *the ghost* . . .

It wasn't a traditional painter's smock that Madame Jonker was wearing, more of a Dominican monk's habit, the fabric as thick and soft as a bathrobe.

The Dutchman's wife also wore a white turban of the same fabric around her head.

She was holding a palette in her left hand, a brush in her right, and her black eyes lighted on Maigret with curiosity.

'I've heard a lot about you, Monsieur Maigret, and I'm delighted to meet you. Forgive me for not shaking hands.'

She put the brush down and wiped her hand on the white robe, where it left green smears.

'I hope you're not an art connoisseur . . . If you are, please don't look at what I'm doing . . .'

Maigret was surprised, after walking past so many masterpieces on the walls, to find himself standing in front of a canvas on which there was nothing but daubs.

5. The Room Covered in Graffiti

In that instant, something happened that Maigret would have been incapable of defining, a change of tone, or rather a sort of shift that suddenly lent more weight to gestures, words and attitudes. Did this stem from the presence of the young woman, still draped in her strange costume, or from the atmosphere of the room?

Logs were burning and crackling in the vast white stone fireplace, and the flames seemed to be leaping sprites.

Maigret now understood why the studio curtains that could be seen from Marinette Augier's windows were nearly always drawn. The studio wasn't only glazed on one side but two, which made it possible to choose the light required.

These curtains were made of thick, black hessian faded to grey in the wash, and had shrunk, so they no longer closed.

On one side, rooftops were visible as far as Saint-Ouen; on the other, with the sails of the Moulin de la Galette in the foreground, lay Paris in almost its entirety, scored by the boulevards, the wider gap of the Champs-Élysées, the curves of the Seine and the gilt dome of Les Invalides.

It was not this panorama that fascinated Maigret, whose senses were sharpened. It is difficult, when suddenly plunged into an unknown milieu, to grasp it fully, and yet that was what seemed to be happening to him.

Everything struck him at once, the two bare walls, for example, painted a glaring white, the dancing flames in the fireplace in the centre of one wall.

Madame Jonker had been busy painting when the two men had come in. Would it not have been natural for there to be canvases on the walls? And also, as in all artists' studios, other canvases stacked against each other? But the varnished wooden floor was as bare as the walls.

Near the easel was a box full of tubes of paint on a pedestal table.

On another table further away, a white-wood table, the only everyday object seen so far in the house, was a jumble of pots, tin cans, bottles and rags.

The rest of the furniture comprised two antique cupboards, a chair and an armchair whose brown velvet upholstery had begun to fade.

Something was not quite right. It was only a hunch, but he was on the alert, and the Dutchman's words only struck him more forcefully. He said, addressing his wife:

'Inspector Maigret isn't here to admire my paintings, but, strange as it may seem, to give a lecture on jealousy. He appears surprised that not all women are jealous . . .'

That could have passed as an unremarkable comment, with a hint of sarcasm. But Maigret understood it as a warning Jonker was giving his wife, and he could have sworn that she acknowledged the message by batting her eyelids.

'Is your wife jealous, Monsieur Maigret?'

'I confess, madame, that she has not yet given me the occasion to ask myself the question.'

'But many women must visit your office?'

Was he mistaken? He thought he detected some sort of signal, but a signal that was for his benefit this time.

So much so that he racked his brains and asked himself if he had ever seen the woman now in front of him at Quai des Orfèvres. Their eyes met. Her lovely face still wore the vague, polite smile of the mistress of the house receiving a guest. But could he not read something else in her huge brown eyes with long fluttering eyelashes?

'Please don't stop working on my account,' he muttered . . .

Because she put the palette down on the pedestal table, removed the white fabric wound round her head like a turban and tossed her head to give her black hair back its shape.

'You are French-born, I believe?'

'Norris told you so?'

The question was natural, ordinary. Was he wrong to perceive a hidden undertone?

'I knew it before coming here.'

'So you made inquiries about us?'

Jonker was less nonchalant than when he had been in his downstairs study and when, his manner slightly sardonic, he had hurried Maigret around the various rooms like a museum or chateau guide.

'Are you tired, darling? Do you want to go and lie down?'

Another signal? An order?

She removed the white hooded robe enveloping her

and emerged in a tight-fitting black dress. Suddenly she looked taller, revealing a curvaceous figure that had reached a delightful maturity.

'Have you been painting for long, madame?'

Instead of replying directly, she explained:

'It's hard to live in a house full of artworks, with a husband whose only passion is paintings, without being tempted to wield a brush. Since I can't compete with the masters I see in front of me from morning till night, I had to content myself with abstract painting. Whatever you do, don't ask me what my daubs represent . . .'

The years spent in England and Paris had not completely eradicated her southern accent, and Maigret was increasingly attentive to the slightest nuances.

'You were born in Nice?'

'You were told that as well?'

Looking her straight in the eye, it was his turn to send her a signal.

'I'm very fond of the Cathedral of Sainte-Réparate . . .'

She didn't blush but gave an imperceptible sign that she had got the message.

'I see you know the city . . .'

With those words he had just evoked the old town of Nice, the poorest neighbourhood with narrow streets where the sun rarely penetrated and washing was strung between the buildings all year round.

He was almost certain now that that was where she had been born, in one of those decrepit houses into which fifteen or twenty families were crammed and whose staircases and courtyards teemed with hordes of brats.

It even seemed to him that she was implicitly admitting it by her attitude and that the two of them had just exchanged something akin to a masonic gesture, in front of the husband, who was oblivious to these subtleties.

Maigret may well have been divisional chief inspector and head of the Police Judiciaire Crime Squad, but he was still of the people.

She may well be living surrounded by paintings worthy of the Louvre, be dressed by the top couturiers, have appeared at society events in Manchester and London adorned with diamonds, rubies and emeralds, but she had still grown up in the shadow of Sainte-Réparate, and he wouldn't have been surprised to learn that she had sold flowers on the café terraces of Place Masséna.

Now they were both playing their parts, as if beneath the words they spoke were others, which were no business of the Dutch banker's son.

'Did your husband build this magnificent studio for you?'

'Oh! No . . . When he built this house, he didn't know me . . . He had a very dear woman friend who was a real painter, unlike me, and who still exhibits in art galleries . . . I wonder why he didn't marry her . . . She probably wasn't young enough? . . . What do you say, Norris?'

'I don't remember . . .'

'You see how polite and tactful he is!'

'I asked you earlier if you had been painting for long.'

'I don't know . . . A few months . . .'

'Do you spend part of your days in this studio?'

'This is a real interrogation,' she joked. 'It's obvious

from your question that you aren't a woman and mistress of a house . . . If you were to ask me, for example, what I did yesterday at such-and-such a time, I would probably find it hard to reply . . . I am lazy . . . and I'm sure that for lazy people, the days go faster than for others, even though others would claim the opposite.'

'I get up late . . . I linger . . . I chat to my maid . . . The cook needs my instructions . . . Lunchtime comes round and I don't even feel I've begun to live . . .'

'You're talking a lot, darling . . .'

And Maigret:

'What I didn't know was that it was possible to paint at night . . .'

This time, there was no doubt that the Jonkers exchanged a look. The husband answered first.

'Perhaps that applied to the Impressionists because what interested them was the play of sunlight, but I know modern painters who consider that artificial light intensifies the colours by several tones . . .'

'Is that why you paint at night, madame?'

'I paint when I feel like it.'

'And you feel like it after dinner, remaining at your easel until two o'clock in the morning . . .'

She tried to smile.

'Well, you certainly seem to know everything there is to know . . .'

He pointed to the black curtain across the bay window overlooking Avenue Junot.

'That curtain, as you can see, does not close completely. I have noticed that in every street, there's at least one person suffering from insomnia. I was talking to your husband about it earlier. The more cultured read or listen to music. Others gaze out of the window . . .'

Jonker now left his wife in charge of operations, as if he were no longer on his own territory. Anxious, he pretended to be only half listening to the conversation and, two or three times, went to stand in front of the panorama of Paris.

The sky was growing paler and paler, turning an increasingly luminous white, especially in the west, where it was almost possible to see the sun going down.

'Are your paintings in these cupboards?'

'No . . . Do you want to check? . . . I don't mind your being nosy . . . After all, you're doing your job.'

She opened one of the cupboards, which contained a jumble of rolls of drawing paper, tubes of paint, more bottles and tin cans like those on the table.

In the second cupboard there was nothing but three blank canvases with the label of a shop in Rue Lepic.

'Are you disappointed? Did you hope to find a skeleton?'

She was alluding to the English saying that every family has a skeleton in the cupboard.

'It takes a long time for a body to become a skeleton,' he replied with a frown. 'For the time being, Lognon is still in a hospital bed . . .'

'Who are you talking about? What a funny name!'

'An inspector . . .'

'The one who was attacked last night?'

'Are you certain, madame, that you were in your bedroom when the shot was fired, the three shots, to be exact?'

'Monsieur Maigret,' Jonker broke in, 'I think that now you're going too far . . .'

'In that case, answer me yourself. Madame Jonker spends part of her time painting, especially in the evenings and often late into the night . . . But I find her in a studio that is almost empty.'

'Is there a French law that makes it obligatory to furnish a studio?'

'One might expect, at the very least, to find a certain number of paintings here, finished or unfinished . . . What do you do with your works, madame?'

Did not the signal she sent her husband mean that she was leaving it up to him to reply?

'Mirella has no pretensions of being an artist . . .'

He heard her first name for the first time. In the past, she must have been called Mireille.

'She generally destroys her works as soon as they are finished—'

'One moment, Monsieur Jonker . . . I apologize once again for appearing finicky . . . I have spent time with painters . . . If they destroy a painting, how do they do it?'

'They cut it up, burn it or throw it in the dustbin . . .'

'But before that?'

'I don't understand.'

'I am surprised, given that you are such a great art lover. Are you saying they throw away the frame as well? . . . Now there are three frames in that cupboard, all of them new . . .'

'My wife sometimes gives the paintings she is the least dissatisfied with to friends . . .'

'Are they the ones that someone comes and collects in the evenings?'

'In the evenings or during the day . . .'

'If it is a question of your wife's works, then she is more prolific than she led me to believe.'

'There are others . . .'

'Do you still need me?' asked Madame Jonker. 'Why don't we go downstairs? I'll have some tea served.'

'Not right away, madame. Your husband was kind enough to show me around the house, but he hasn't shown me what is behind that door yet . . .'

A solid dark oak door, at the back of the studio.

'Who knows? We might at last find some of your paintings.'

There was a tension, electricity in the air. Their voices became more muted, more trenchant.

'I'm afraid not, Monsieur Maigret.'

'Why are you so certain?'

'Because that door hasn't been opened for months, if not years . . . It used to be the bedroom of the person my wife mentioned, let us say the room where she would rest between painting bouts . . .'

'And you preserve it like a sanctuary? After all these years?'

He attacked deliberately, to make his adversary lose his cool. He felt the moment had come to drive home his advantage, and, this time, exceptionally, the scene was not taking place in his office at Quai des Orfèvres but in an artist's studio with a panoramic view of Paris.

Jonker's fists were clenched, but he still maintained his composure.

'I am convinced, Monsieur Maigret, that if I were to turn up at your home unannounced, if I were to search high and low, if I asked your wife question upon question, I would find many details of your private life strange, if not inexplicable. You see, each one of us has our own way of thinking and behaviour which others find incomprehensible.

'This house is fairly large. I devote myself almost entirely to my paintings . . . Our social life is very limited, and my wife, as she told you, casually occupies herself by painting . . . Is it surprising that she does not attach a great deal of importance to what happens to her canvases, whether she burns them, throws them in the dustbin or gives them to friends?'

'What friends?'

'I am obliged to answer your question as I already did in my study. It would not be very gentlemanly of me to be indiscreet and expose others to the unpleasantness we have been caused by shots fired in our street by strangers . . .'

'To go back to that door . . .'

'I don't know how many rooms your apartment has, Monsieur Maigret. This house has thirty-two. Four servants come and go. It has happened that a maid has been fired for dishonesty . . .'

'That a key should get lost under these conditions will not surprise anyone in our circles . . .'

'And you didn't have a new one made?'

'It didn't occur to me.'

'Are you certain that the key is not in the house?'

'Not to my knowledge . . . If it is, one of these days we will find it in the most unexpected place.'

'May I use this telephone?'

Because there was a handset on the table. Maigret had noticed that there was one in most rooms, probably for both external and internal communications.

'What do you intend to do?'

'Call a locksmith.'

'I don't think I would agree to that because it seems to me that you are going beyond your remit . . .'

'Then I shall call the public prosecutor, who will send me an official search warrant.'

The husband and wife exchanged glances again. It was Mirella who went over to the cupboard, carrying the stool she had taken from next to the easel. She clambered on to it, swept her hand across the top of the cupboard and, when she withdrew it, she was holding a key.

'You see, Monsieur Jonker, there was one detail that struck me, or rather two connected details. The door to this studio has a lock, but, unusually, this lock is on the outside.

'Earlier, while you were speaking, I noticed that it is the same with this door . . .'

'You are at liberty to be surprised, Monsieur Maigret, and you have been continually since you entered this house. Your lifestyle and ours are too different for you to be able to understand . . .'

'I am making an effort, you see . . .'

Maigret took the key that Madame Jonker was holding out to him and walked over to the locked door. While the couple stood rooted to the spot in the vast studio like two waxworks, he jiggled the lock.

'How long did you say it is since this door has been opened?'

'It doesn't matter.'

'I'll allow you to keep your distance, madame, and you can imagine why, but I would like your husband to come here . . .'

Jonker walked towards the door, trying to keep up appearances.

'You will notice first of all that this floor is clean, without a trace of dust, and if you touch it, you will see that in places the wood is still damp, as if it had recently been thoroughly scrubbed . . . Who cleaned this room, this morning or last night?'

He heard Mirella's voice behind him reply:

'It certainly wasn't me . . . You can ask the maids . . . Unless Carl was given instructions by my husband . . .'

The room was not large. Like the bay window in the studio, the window afforded a panoramic view of Paris, and the old floral curtains were paint-stained. In places, it even looked as if someone had wiped their hands on them after painting with their fingers.

In a corner was an iron bedstead with a mattress but no sheets or blankets.

The most striking thing was what can only be described as graffiti. On the grubby white walls were obscene drawings of the kind found on the walls of some urinals. The difference was that instead of being drawn in pencil, they had been done with paint – green, blue, yellow and purple.

'I won't ask you, Monsieur Jonker, if you attribute these drawings to your former friend . . . But there's one that makes this hypothesis indeed impossible . . .'

It was, in a few thick brush-strokes, a portrait of Mirella, more animated than many of the paintings in the drawing room.

'Do you expect an explanation?'

'I think that would be normal. Our lifestyles, as you said, may be very different. It is possible that I find your behaviour a little hard to understand. All the same, I am convinced that even your friends, people from your world, would be very surprised to discover these . . . er! . . . these . . . shall we call them frescos beneath your roof.'

Not only were there very detailed depictions of the parts of the human body that are usually concealed, but there were scenes of unbridled eroticism. In contrast, close to the bed, vertical strokes reminded Maigret of the ones that prisoners drew to keep track of time.

'Was the person living here counting the days with such impatience?'

'I don't understand.'

'You were not unaware of the existence of these graffiti?'

'I glanced around this room a long time ago . . .'

'How long?'

'Several months, I told you . . . I was shocked by what I saw and after double-locking the door, I threw the key on top of the cupboard . . .'

'In front of your wife?'

'I don't remember . . .'

'Do you know what is on the walls of this room, madame?'

She nodded.

'How did you feel when you saw your portrait?'

'I don't call that a portrait but a vague sketch, like any painter can hastily draw . . .'

'I'm waiting for you two to agree on what to tell me.'

There was a silence, and Maigret took his pipe from his pocket without being invited to do so.

'I wonder,' muttered Jonker, 'whether it might not be better for me to call my lawyer. I am not familiar enough with French law to know whether you have the right to question us like this.'

'If, instead of giving me a plausible reply straight away, you call your lawyer, tell him to come to Quai des Orfèvres because, in that case, I'm taking you there this instant.'

'Without a warrant?'

'With or without a warrant. If necessary, the warrant will be here in half an hour.'

Maigret went over to the telephone.

'Wait!'

'Who occupied that room?'

'It is ancient history . . . Do you not want to go downstairs and continue this conversation over a drink? I wouldn't mind smoking a cigar and I don't have any on me.'

'On condition that Madame Jonker accompanies us.'

She walked ahead, with a weary step, as if resigned. Then came Maigret, with Jonker close behind.

'Here?' asked Mirella when they reached the drawing room.

'I prefer my study.'

'What can I offer you, Monsieur Maigret?'

'Nothing for the time being.'

She saw the glass he had drunk from earlier, which was still on the desk with her husband's. Did Maigret's refusal not indicate that the situation had changed?

It was darker in the room, and Jonker switched on the lamps, poured himself some Curaçao and shot his wife a questioning look.

'No. I'd rather have a whisky.'

He was the first to sit down, replicating almost exactly the pose he'd adopted an hour earlier. His wife remained standing, holding her glass.

'Two or three years ago—' began the art lover, cutting off the end of his cigar.

Maigret broke in:

'Have you noticed that you are never precise? Since I've been here, you have not once given a date or a name, other than names of long-dead painters . . . You speak of a few weeks, a few months, a few years, early or late evening . . .'

'Maybe because I do not concern myself with time? Remember I don't have to keep office hours and, until today, I have never had to give an account of myself to anyone.'

He was becoming aggressive again, his exaggerated disdain ringing false. Maigret caught, on his wife's face, an expression of anxiety, of disapproval.

'You, my dear,' he thought, 'you know from experience that there's no point playing that little game with the police . . .'

Was it in Nice, in her youth, that she'd had dealings with the law, or was it in England, or elsewhere?

'You are free to believe me or not, Monsieur Maigret . . . I repeat that two or three years ago, I was told about a talented young painter who was living in such dire straits that he sometimes slept in the street and rummaged through the dustbins for food.'

'You say you were told about this young man. Was it by a friend or by an art dealer?'

Jonker made as if brushing away a fly.

'What does it matter! I don't remember. The fact was I was ashamed to have this studio that served no purpose—'

'So your wife didn't paint at the time?'

'No . . . I wouldn't have invited him here . . .'

'What is the name of this graffiti artist?'

'I only ever knew his first name—'

'Which is?'

A pause:

'Pedro.'

He was visibly lying.

'A Spaniard? An Italian?'

'Do you know, I didn't bother to find out. I allowed him to use the studio and the bedroom. I gave him money to buy paints and canvases.'

'And, at night, you locked him in to stop him gallivanting?'

'I didn't lock him in.'

'Why, in that case, the external locks?'

'They were fitted when the house was built.'

'For what reason?'

'A very simple reason. It hasn't occurred to you because you are not a collector. For a long time, in that studio I stored the paintings I had no room for on the walls . . . It made sense to lock them in from outside, since it wasn't possible to do so from the inside.'

'I thought the studio had been built for your painter girlfriend at the time . . .'

'Let us say that the locks were fitted once she no longer lived here . . .'

'Including on the bedroom door?'

'I am not even certain I told the locksmith to fit one on that door . . .'

'To return to Pedro . . .'

'He lived in the house for several months.'

'*Several!*' emphasized Maigret, whereas Mirella couldn't help smiling.

Jonker was growing impatient and he must have had extraordinary self-control not to let his anger erupt.

'Was he talented?'

'Very.'

'Did he make a career? Did he become famous?'

'I don't know . . . I went up to the studio a number of times and I admired his paintings—'

'Did you buy any?'

'How could I buy paintings from a man I was providing with board and lodging?'

'So you do not own a single one of his works? . . . It didn't occur to him to give you one before he left?'

'Have you seen any paintings in the house that are less than thirty years old? . . . An art lover is often a collector . . . and each collector confines himself to a specific period . . . I, for instance, start with Van Gogh and end with Modigliani.'

'Did Pedro have his meals up there?'

'I suppose so.'

'Did Carl take them up to him?'

'My wife dealt with those details.'

'It was Carl,' she replied in a hollow voice.

'Did he go out a lot?'

'Like all young men of his age.'

'How old was he, as a matter of fact?'

'Twenty-two or twenty-three. He ended up finding male and female friends. At first, he only brought one or two to the studio at a time. Then he went too far. Some nights there were twenty or so of them making a great disturbance just above my wife's apartment, which kept her awake—'

'You never had the curiosity to go up and find out what was going on, madame?'

'My husband took care of it.'

'And the result was?'

'He threw Pedro out, not without giving him some money.'

'Was that when you discovered the graffiti?'

Jonker nodded.

'You too, madame? In that case, your portrait must have

revealed that Pedro was in love with you. Did he ever make a pass at you?'

'If you continue in this vein, Monsieur Maigret, I will regretfully have to inform my ambassador of your way of going about things,' said Jonker harshly.

'Will you also tell him about the people who slip into the house at night and spend part or all of the night here?'

'I thought I knew the French . . .'

'I thought I knew the Dutch . . .'

Mirella interrupted:

'Why don't you two stop arguing? I understand that my husband is annoyed at being asked certain questions, especially when they're about me. I also understand the difficulty for inspector Maigret to accept our lifestyle . . .

'As regards those women, Monsieur Maigret, I've always known about them, even before we were married . . . You would be surprised at the number of husbands in the same situation . . . Most of them keep it secret, especially in conventional circles . . . Norris prefers to be open, and I see it as a tribute to my intelligence and my affection.'

He noted that she did not say 'love'.

'I think the fact that he has nothing to hide explains why some of his replies have been vague and the apparent contradictions—'

'So I am going to ask you a very precise question. Until what time did you stay in the studio last night?'

'I need to think, because I don't bother with wearing a watch when I work, and you will have noticed there is no clock up there . . . At around eleven o'clock I sent my personal maid to bed—'

'You were on the second floor?'

'Yes. She came and asked me if she should wait up for me to help me get ready for bed—'

'Were you working on the painting that is still on the easel?'

'I spent a long time, charcoal in one hand, a rag in the other, trying to think of a subject.'

'What is the subject of this work?'

'Let's call it a harmony ... Abstract painting isn't haphazard ... Maybe it demands more reflection and trial and error than figurative painting—'

'We were talking about times ...'

'It could have been one o'clock in the morning when I went downstairs to my apartment.'

'Did you switch the studio light off?'

'I think so. It's a reflex.'

'Were you wearing the same white garment and turban as you're wearing today?'

'To be honest, it's an old bathrobe and a terry-towel. Since I only paint to amuse myself, it would have felt ridiculous buying a professional artist's smock—'

'Was your husband in bed? Did you not go and wish him good night?'

'I don't normally do that when I go to bed after him.'

'For fear of finding him in the company of one of his female visitors?'

'If you like.'

'I think we're getting to the end ...'

He felt the atmosphere in the room relax, but this was an old trick of his. He slowly re-lit his pipe and appeared to be racking his brains to make sure he hadn't forgotten anything.

'Earlier, Monsieur Jonker, you pointed out, not without tact, that I know nothing about the thinking and actions of an art lover. I see, from your bookshelves, that you follow the major auctions. And you buy a lot, because at one point you had to store in the studio paintings for which you had no space anywhere else . . .

'Should I infer that you sell the works you no longer like?'

'I am going to try, once and for all, to explain. I inherited a certain number of paintings from my father, who was not only a renowned financier, but also one of the first to discover artists whose works the museums now vie with one another to purchase.

'My income, although substantial, did not permit me to buy the paintings I fancied ad infinitum.

'Like all collectors, I began with second-best pieces, let us call them minor works, by great artists . . .

'Gradually, as they gained in value and my taste developed, I sold some of these works to buy more important ones—'

'I'm sorry to interrupt you. You continued until recently?'

'I intend to continue until I die.'

'These paintings that you sell, do you send them to the Drouot auction house, or do you entrust them to an art dealer?'

'I have, on rare occasions, put a painting or two up for public auction. However, the works sold at auction generally come from an estate. A connoisseur prefers to go about things differently.'

'Meaning?'

'He knows the market. He knows, for example, that such-and-such a museum in the USA or in South America is looking for a Renoir, a Picasso from the Blue Period. If he wants to sell a painting of that kind, he makes contacts . . .'

'That would explain why neighbours saw paintings leaving your house . . . ?'

'Those and my wife's . . .'

'Can you, Monsieur Jonker, provide me with the names of some of your buyers? Let's take only the past year, for example . . .'

'No.'

It was a cold, emphatic no.

'Must I conclude that it is a matter of smuggling?'

'I don't like that word. Operations of this kind are carried out with discretion. Most countries, for example, regulate the export of artworks to protect their national heritage.

'Not only do the museums have a right of pre-emption, but an export licence is often refused.

'In the drawing room you can see one of the first works of De Chirico which was smuggled across the Italian border, as well as a Manet which, unbelievable as it may seem, came from Russia.

'Do you understand why I cannot give names? Someone buys a painting from me. I deliver it to the purchaser. He pays me, and I don't have to worry about what happens to it . . .'

'You don't know?'

'I don't want to know. It's none of my business. Any more than it is to find out about the provenance of a painting that I buy . . .'

Maigret rose. He felt as if he had been in that house for ever and the muffled, almost unreal atmosphere was becoming oppressive. What was more, he was thirsty, but given the point he and Jonker had reached, he was no longer entitled to accept a drink.

'I apologize, madame, for having interrupted your work and ruined your afternoon . . .'

Did Mirella's eyes not contain a question?

'It's not over, is it?' she seemed to be saying. 'I know police methods. You're not going to let go of us and I wonder what trick you've got up your sleeve . . .'

Turning towards her husband, she hesitated, opened her mouth and went back over to Maigret to murmur tritely:

'Delighted to have met you.'

Jonker, on his feet, crushing the end of his cigar in the ashtray, said:

'I am sorry I did not always keep my cool . . . One should never forget one's duties as a host . . .'

They didn't ring for Carl to show him out, but Jonker preceded him in person to the front door, which he opened. Outside, the cool air had a taste of damp and dust. A halo was beginning to form around the streetlamps.

On the opposite side of the street, Marinette Augier's windows were dark. There was no light on the first floor of the neighbouring building either, but an old man's face was pressed to the windowpane.

Maigret nearly gave a friendly wave to old Maclet stalwartly keeping watch. He was even tempted to go and knock on his door, but more urgent matters awaited him.

That did not stop him, before climbing into a taxi on the corner of Rue Caulaincourt, from going into the bar he'd been in that morning and downing two beers in quick succession.

6. The Barefoot Drunkard

Habits form quickly in neighbourhood bars. Because he had drunk a grog that morning, the owner in his shirt-sleeves looked surprised when his customer ordered a beer. And when Maigret requested a telephone token, he asked:

'Just one?'

The person who had used the booth before Maigret had drunk a serious amount of calvados, because the air reeked of it and even the handset smelled of apple brandy.

'Hello! Who's that?'

'Inspector Neveu.'

'Is Lucas not in the office?'

'I'll call him . . . Just a moment . . . He's on another line . . .'

Maigret waited patiently, gazing absently at the soothing décor of the little café, its pewter counter and its familiar bottles and labels. The newspapers talked with complacency or anxiety about a world that was changing at breakneck speed but here, before his eyes, after all these years and a world war, were the same bottle labels that he used to see in the village inn as a child.

'Sorry, chief . . .'

'I want the house of a certain Norris Jonker, in Avenue Junot, put under surveillance as soon as possible. It's opposite the building Lognon came out of when he was shot. Put at least two men and a car there . . .'

'I'm not sure there are any left in the yard. I fear there aren't—'

'Find one . . . Not only must the Jonkers be followed if they leave the house, but visitors must also be tailed . . . Get a move on . . .'

In the taxi weaving through the lights, he felt in a strange mood. He should have been pleased with himself, because he hadn't been intimidated by the Dutchman's arrogance and wealth, or by Mirella's dazzling beauty.

Rarely had he gathered so many details in a single day about a case he'd had no inkling of on getting up that morning. Not only had the art lover's house come alive and yielded a number of little secrets, but Avenue Junot, which he thought he knew, had taken on a new countenance.

Why did he feel dissatisfied with himself and vaguely worried? He asked himself the question and tried to answer it, but it was only as the taxi was crossing the Pont-au-Change and he glimpsed the familiar outline of the old Palais de Justice that he believed he'd identified the cause of his unease.

Although he had spent most of his time in Norris Jonker's study, had visited the house from top to bottom, and the most dramatic scene had taken place in the second-floor studio, his strongest memory was not of those places.

The image that stayed with him, as obstinate as a tune on the brain, was that of the little bedroom with an iron bedstead, and he suddenly understood the reason for his concern.

Like in a film close-up, he saw those obscene images again, drawn on the white walls, with broad brush-strokes, in red, black and blue. When he tried to picture Mirella Jonker, it was her portrait in a few hastily drawn lines that stood out most in his mind.

Was not the person who had created that image in a frenzy, surrounding it with wild sexual symbols, mad? Did not the drawings of lunatics that he'd had the occasion to see exude that same energy and evocative power?

The room had been occupied recently, that was beyond doubt. Why, otherwise, would it have been thoroughly scrubbed down in the past few hours? And why had they not dared repaint the walls white?

He lumbered up the main staircase of the Police Judiciaire. Instead of going directly to his office, he first dropped into the inspectors' room, as was his habit. Under the globe lights, each person was working at their desk, like students at an evening class.

He didn't look at anyone in particular, but he found it comforting to be back in touch with headquarters and its professional atmosphere.

They did not raise their eyes any more than pupils do when the teacher walks past; yet they all knew that he was grave and anxious, that his face bore signs not just of weariness but of exhaustion.

'My wife hasn't called?'

'No, chief.'

'Phone her at home. If she's not there, try Lognon's number.'

. . . Perhaps not an actual madman, not someone who should be locked up in a psychiatric hospital, but someone violent, unable to control his instincts . . .

'Hello! Is that you?'

She was back at their apartment and was probably busy cooking dinner.

'Have you been home long?'

'Over an hour. To be honest, I don't think she particularly wants me there . . . She was flattered that I took the trouble, but she doesn't feel comfortable with me . . . She far prefers the company of the old dear with the rosary . . . The pair of them can complain to their hearts' content and count their endless woes . . .

'I went and bought a few treats from the local shops . . . I slipped a banknote into the hand of the old woman, who didn't bat an eyelid, and I promised to drop in tomorrow . . .

'What about you? Do you plan to be here for dinner?'

'I don't know yet. I doubt it.'

'How's Lognon?'

'The last I heard, he was alive, but I've only just got back to the office . . .'

'See you tonight, I hope . . .'

'See you tonight . . .'

He didn't call her by her first name, nor she him. They didn't call one another 'darling'. What would be the point, since they felt almost like one and the same person?

He hung up and opened the door.

'Is Janvier there?'

'Coming, chief . . .'

And Maigret, sitting at his desk, on which he kept his pipes:

'Lognon, first . . .'

'I telephoned the hospital ten minutes ago . . . The matron is losing patience . . . Condition stable . . . The doctors aren't expecting any change before tomorrow at the earliest . . . He's in a coma and, even if his eyes open, he doesn't know where he is, who is beside him or what happened to him . . .'

'Have you seen Marinette Augier's ex-fiancé?'

'I found him at his office and he seemed frightened at the thought that his father might have found out I was from the police . . . The father, apparently, is a harsh man who terrifies his staff . . . Jean-Claude, on the other hand, is a spineless fop, a weakling . . . He dragged me outside and put on an act in front of the young lady in reception, passing me off as a client . . .'

'What do they manufacture?'

'Metal pipes of I don't know what – copper, iron or cast iron. It's a big, sinister place of the sort you find around Avenue de la République and Boulevard Voltaire . . . He took me to a café, a long way from the office . . . The afternoon papers are full of the shooting and Lognon's injuries, but don't mention Marinette . . . Jean-Claude hadn't read them, incidentally . . .'

'Was he cooperative?'

'He's so frightened of his father and, in general, of anything that might complicate his life, that he would have confessed all his youthful sins . . . I told him that Marinette had suddenly left her home and that we urgently needed her witness statement . . .

'"You were engaged for nearly a year . . ."

'"Engaged, well . . . That's a bit of an exaggeration . . ."

'"Or an understatement, since you used to spend one or two nights a week at her place . . ."

'It really annoyed him that we knew.

'"Anyhow, if she's expecting a baby, it can't be mine, because we haven't seen one another for over nine months . . ."

'You see the type, chief! I asked him about their weekends.

'"You must have had favourite places where you used to go . . . Do you have a car?"

'"Of course."

'"Did you go to the seaside or did you stay in the Paris region?"

'"In the Paris region . . . Not always the same spot . . . We'd choose an inn, nearly always by the river, because Marinette was crazy about swimming and canoeing . . . She didn't like hotels, elegant and sophisticated places . . . To be honest, her tastes were very common . . ."

'I managed to get half a dozen addresses out of him, those of the spots they went to several times, the Auberge du Clou, in Courcelles, in the Chevreuse valley, Chez Mélanie, in Saint-Fargeau, between Corbeil and Melun, Félix et Félicie, in Pomponne . . . It's beside the Marne, not far from Lagny . . . She was especially fond of that bistro, because it's just a rural café with two guest rooms and no running water . . .

'Then Créguy, near Meaux, an open-air dance hall whose name he can't remember and whose owner is deaf . . . The Pie-qui-Danse, in the middle of the country-side between Meulan and Apremont . . . They ate only once at the Coq-Hardi, in Bougival . . .'

'Have you checked?'

'I thought I'd do better staying here and gathering the intelligence. I could have phoned the local police in the various villages, but I was afraid they might give the game away and cause the young lady to run away . . . It's not very regular, given that these places are outside our patch, but I understood you were in a hurry . . .'

'Well?'

'I sent a man in each direction, Lourtie, Jamin and Lagrume . . .'

'Did they each take a car?'

'Yes,' admitted Janvier anxiously.

'Is that why Lucas has just told me that there are probably no cars available?'

'I'm sorry . . .'

'You did well . . . No results yet?'

'Only from the Auberge du Clou . . . Nothing there . . . The others will be reporting back soon . . .'

Maigret smoked his pipe in silence, as if he'd forgotten Janvier's presence.

'Do you still need me here?'

'Not for the time being. Don't go off without informing me, though. Tell Lucas to stay as well . . .'

He wanted to move fast. After his long visit to the Dutchman that afternoon, he felt that someone was in danger, while remaining incapable of saying who was at risk.

Of course, they'd contrived to show him a façade. While the paintings on the walls were authentic, wasn't everything else he'd seen and heard false?

'Get me Immigration . . .'

It only took ten minutes or so for him to obtain Madame Jonker's maiden name. Her first name wasn't Mireille, as he had thought because of Mirella and her southern roots, but the very ordinary Marcelle, and her surname had been Maillant.

'Get hold of the Nice Police Judiciaire, will you. Preferably Detective Chief Inspector Bastiani . . .'

Unable to remain idle, he was casting around at random in all directions.

'Hello! Bastiani? How are you, my old friend? . . . Like the weather? . . . Here it's been raining for the past three days and it's only let up since midday, but the sky's still grey . . . Listen, I'd like your men to search through some old paperwork quickly . . . If you've got nothing, they could try at the Palais de Justice. It's concerning a certain Marcelle Maillant, born in Nice, probably in the old town, in the Sainte-Réparate neighbourhood . . .'

'She's thirty-four. After her marriage to an Englishman by the name of Muir, who manufactures ball-bearings in Manchester, she lived in London for a number of years, where she married a wealthy Dutchman, Norris Jonker, and she currently lives in Paris . . .'

'A magnificent woman, the kind who turns heads in the street . . . Tall, dark-haired, elegantly dressed . . . Very much a woman of the world, but with a little something that niggles me . . . Do you know what I mean? . . . Something's not quite right, I don't know what but the way she looked at me confirms it . . .'

'Yes, it's really urgent . . . I'd swear that something

ugly's going to happen and I'd like to prevent it . . . By the way, did you ever meet Lognon, when you were at the Sûreté? . . . Old Hard-Done-By, that's right . . . He was shot last night . . . He's not dead, but no one can be sure he'll recover . . . It's to do with this case, yes . . . I'm not sure how or to what extent she's mixed up in it, but your intelligence may shed some light . . .

'I'm staying in my office . . . All night if I have to . . .'

He knew that on learning that the investigation concerned a colleague who had been shot, Bastiani and his men would pull out all the stops. For them it was a point of honour.

For a good five minutes, he appeared to be daydreaming, dozing, then his arm reached for the telephone.

'I'd like to be put through to Scotland Yard . . . As a matter of urgency . . . Inspector Pyke . . . One moment . . . No! Chief Inspector Pyke . . .'

They had met in France, where the worthy Inspector Pyke had come to study the methods of the Police Judiciaire, and of Maigret especially, and had been surprised to discover that Maigret had no method at all.

They had seen one another twice more in London and had become good friends. A few months earlier, Maigret had learned that Pyke had earned more stripes.

Although he was put through to Scotland Yard in three minutes, it took another ten before Pyke was on the other end, and a few more to exchange congratulations in bad English on Maigret's part and in bad French on Pyke's.

'. . . Maillant, yes . . . *M* for Maurice, *A* for André . . .'

He had to spell out the names.

'. . . Muir . . . M for Maurice again . . . U for Ursula . . .'

'I know that name . . . Is it Sir Herbert Muir? . . . Of Manchester? . . . The Queen knighted him three years ago . . .'

'Second husband: Norris Jonker . . .'

He spelled out the name again, mentioning the Dutchman's stint in the British army, his rank of colonel.

'There were perhaps other men between the two . . . Apparently she lived for a while in London, where I doubt she remained alone . . .'

Maigret took care to add that it was a case of a police officer being attacked, and Mr Pyke declared gravely:

'Here the culprit would be hanged, man or woman. Those guilty of killing police officers are always hanged . . .'

Like Bastiani, he promised to call back.

It was half past six. When he opened the communicating door, Maigret found only four or five inspectors left in the big office.

'Nothing at Chez Mélanie, in Saint-Fargeau, chief. Nothing either at the Coq-Hardi, as I expected, or at the Pie-qui-Danse . . . There's just the Marne left, since I drew a blank with the Chevreuse valley and Seine areas.'

Maigret was about to go back into his office when Inspector Chinquier came into the room in a state of great agitation.

'Is the chief here?'

He spotted Maigret before the words were out of his mouth.

'I've got news . . . Rather than phoning you from the office, I preferred to dash over myself . . .'

'Come in . . .'

'I've left a witness in the waiting room, in case you want to question him.'

'First, sit down and tell me . . .'

'May I remove my coat? I've raced around so much today that I'm drenched in sweat . . . That's better! . . . As you requested, the men from the eighteenth have gone through Avenue Junot and the surrounding streets with a fine-tooth comb . . . For hours, apart from old Maclet, it proved fruitless . . . Then, suddenly, I was given some information that seemed to me to be of the utmost . . .

'We'd already been to that apartment building in the early afternoon and questioned the concierge and those residents who were at home, not many, mainly women, because the men were at work . . .

'It's an investment property located at the top of the avenue . . .

'Just when one of my colleagues returned there, less than an hour ago, a man went into the lodge to collect his post, a certain Langeron, who's a door-to-door vacuum-cleaner salesman . . . I've brought him in . . .

'He's a rather morose man, more used to being kicked out than welcomed with open arms . . . He lives alone, in an apartment on the third floor, and works irregular hours, always in the hope of catching people at the right moment . . .

'He generally cooks his own meals, but when he makes a sale he treats himself to dinner at a restaurant . . . That's what happened yesterday . . . Between six and eight, when people are usually at home, he sold two vacuum cleaners and, after a drink in a brasserie on Place Clichy, he dined copiously in a little restaurant in Rue Caulaincourt . . .

'Shortly before ten o'clock, he was walking up Avenue Junot carrying his demo vacuum cleaner . . . Outside the Dutchman's house a car was parked, a yellow Jaguar whose number plate struck him because it was marked TT in red letters . . .

'He was just a few metres away when the front door opened—'

'Is he certain that it was the door of the Jonkers' mansion?'

'He knows all the buildings on Avenue Junot inside out because, of course, he tries to sell vacuum cleaners there . . . Listen carefully . . . Two men came out, supporting a third who was so drunk that he could no longer stand on his own feet . . .

'When the two individuals who were virtually carrying the third one to the car spotted Langeron, they made as if to go back into the house, but one of them rebuked the drunk one:

'"Come on! . . . Walk, idiot! . . . What a disgrace you are, getting yourself into such a state!"'

'Did they take him away?'

'Wait. That's not all. First, my vacuum-cleaner salesman states that the man who spoke had a strong English accent . . . Secondly, the drunkard, was wearing neither shoes nor socks . . . Apparently his bare feet were being dragged over the pavement . . . They put him on the rear seat, with one of the men who'd been supporting him, while the other took the wheel . . . The car roared off . . .

'Do you want me to call my man in?'

Maigret hesitated, convinced that there was less and less time to lose.

'Make him comfortable next door and take down his statement. Make sure he leaves nothing out. A detail can prove important . . .'

'Then what do I do?'

'Let's talk about it again when you've finished . . .'

The previous day, at the same time, he had been grilling young Bauche, nicknamed Jeannot, and, at one o'clock in the morning, he had wormed the confession out of him that had enabled him to lock up Gaston Nouveau.

He was beginning to wonder whether, again tonight, the lights in his office would be on until goodness-knows-what hour. That rarely happened twice in a row. Between cases, there was nearly always a pause and, paradoxically, if this pause went on too long, Maigret became bad-tempered and restive.

'Vehicle Registration . . . Quick! . . .'

He didn't recall ever having seen a yellow Jaguar, an unusual colour for an English car. The 'TT' indicated that the car had entered France with a foreign driver who would only be staying in the country for a short time and was exempt from customs duty.

'Who deals with TTs in your department? . . . Rorive? . . . He's not in the office? . . . Everyone's gone home? . . . What about you, you're there, aren't you? . . . Listen, young man . . . You'll simply have to manage . . . Either go into Rorive's office and look for the information I need, or phone him and tell him to come at once . . . It

doesn't matter if he's in the middle of having dinner . . .
Understood? . . . It's about a Jaguar . . . Jaguar, yes . . .

'It was still driving around Paris last night . . . It's yellow
and has a TT plate . . . No! I don't know the number . . .
That would be a fine thing . . . but I presume there aren't
dozens of yellow Jaguars with TT plates in Paris . . .

'Get a move on one way or another and call me at
Quai des Orfèvres with the information . . . The owner's
name, his address, date of arrival in France . . . Hurry
up . . . My apologies to Rorive if you have to disturb
him . . . I'll return the favour . . . Tell him it's about finding the guy who shot Lognon . . . Yes, the inspector from
the eighteenth . . .'

He went and opened the door a fraction to call Janvier.

'Still nothing from the Marne?'

'Not yet. Maybe Lagrume has broken down . . .'

'What time is it?'

'Seven o'clock . . .'

'I'm thirsty . . . Have some beers sent up . . . While
you're about it, I think it might be a good idea to order
some sandwiches . . .'

'For how many?'

'I don't know . . . A heap of sandwiches . . .'

He paced up and down, his hands behind his back, then
ended up reaching for the phone again.

'My wife, please . . .'

To tell her that he definitely wouldn't be home for
dinner.

He had barely hung up when it rang and he hurried over
to pick it up.

'Hello! . . . Yes . . . Bastiani? . . . So it was easier than you expected? . . . Luck? . . . Right! . . . Go on . . .'

He sat at his desk, pulled over a notepad and grabbed a pencil.

'What name did you say? . . . Stanley Hobson . . . What? . . . It's a long story? . . . Make it as short as possible, without leaving anything out . . . But not at all, my friend . . . I'm a bit on edge this evening . . . I'm convinced we've got to move fast . . . There's a barefoot drunkard who's niggling me . . . Right . . . I'm listening . . .'

The case went back sixteen years. A certain Stanley Hobson had been arrested in Nice, in a luxury hotel on the Promenade des Anglais. He had a record at Scotland Yard as a jewellery thief . . . Several jewellery robberies had just been committed in villas in Antibes and Cannes, another in a room at the hotel where Hobson was staying.

At the time of his arrest, he was with a girl who was not quite eighteen and who had been his mistress for several weeks.

She'd been taken to the police station with him and they'd both been questioned for three days. The room had been searched. The police had also searched the home in the old town of Nice of the girl's mother, who worked at the flower market.

No jewellery was found. For lack of proof, the pair were released and, two days later, they crossed over into Italy.

There was no further news in Nice of either Hobson or Marcelle Maillant, because she was indeed the girl in question.

'Do you know what became of the mother?'

'For the past few years she's been living in a comfortable apartment in Rue Saint-Sauveur and she has a private income. I sent one of my men over to her place, but he's not back yet. She probably receives money orders from her daughter . . .'

'Thank you, Bastiani. We'll speak later, I hope . . .'

The wheels were beginning to turn, as Maigret described it, and, at these times, he wished all the offices were open day and night.

'Come here for a moment, Lucas . . . Go down to the Hotel Agency . . . With any luck someone will still be there . . . Note down the name . . . Stanley Hobson . . . According to Bastiani, he'd be between forty-five and forty-eight by now . . . I don't have a description but, over fifteen years ago, Scotland Yard circulated his details to all the police forces as an international jewellery thief . . .'

'Go up to Records if necessary . . . There's a chance they'll have something on him . . .'

With Lucas gone, Maigret looked at the telephone reproachfully, as if he was annoyed with it for not ringing every second. Chinquier knocked on his door.

'There you are, sir. The statement is typed up and Langeron has signed it. He's asking if he may go and have dinner. You really don't want to see him?'

Maigret contented himself with a glance through the half-open door. The individual was ordinary, unassuming.

'Let him go and eat and then come back, just in case. I don't know yet whether I'll need him or when, but too many people have already vanished into thin air . . .'

'What do I do?'

'Aren't you hungry? Don't you ever eat?'

'I'd like to make myself useful . . .'

'It would be best if you went back to the eighteenth and kept me posted on what's happening in the neighbourhood . . .'

'Are you hoping for something?'

'If I weren't, I'd go home and have dinner with my wife in front of the television . . .'

The waiter from the Brasserie Dauphine was still in Maigret's office, where he'd delivered a tray full of glasses of beer and sandwiches, when the telephone rang.

'Good! . . . Well done! . . . Ed? . . . Just Ed? . . . An American? . . . I understand . . . Even their presidents have nicknames . . . Ed Gollan . . . double l? Do you have the address? . . . What?'

Maigret was becoming gloomy. It was about the owner of the yellow Jaguar.

'Are you sure it's the only one there is in Paris? . . . Good! . . . Thank you, my friend . . . I'll see where this leads, but I'd have been happier if he weren't a guest at the Ritz . . .'

He went into the inspectors' office again.

'I need two men to get ready to take cars . . . I hope there are some left down there?'

'Two have just come back.'

A moment later, he was on the phone again.

'The Ritz? . . . Put me through to the concierge, please, mademoiselle . . . Hello! Is that the concierge? . . . Is that you, Pierre? . . . Maigret here . . .'

He had carried out several investigations in the hotel on Place Vendôme, one of the most exclusive, if not the most exclusive, in Paris, and each time he had done so with appropriate discretion.

'The detective chief inspector, yes . . . Listen carefully and don't say any names . . . At this hour the lobby must be full of people . . . Do you have a certain Gollan among your guests? . . . Ed Gollan . . .'

'Just a moment, if you don't mind. I'm going to transfer the call to one of the booths . . .'

Shortly after he confirmed:

'He is staying here, yes. He's a regular guest . . . He's an American, born in San Francisco, who travels a lot and comes to Paris three or four times a year . . . He usually stays around three weeks . . .'

'How old?'

'Thirty-eight . . . Not the businessman type at all but the intellectual type . . . According to his passport, he's an art critic and, so I've been told, an internationally reputed expert . . . He's entertained the director of the Louvre several times, and major art dealers come and see him—'

'Is he in his suite right now?'

'What time is it? . . . Seven thirty? . . . It's highly likely that he'll be in the bar . . .'

'Could you discreetly check?'

Another wait.

'Yes, he's there . . .'

'Alone?'

'With a pretty woman.'

'A hotel guest?'

'She's not quite the sort; he's had a drink with her before and later they'll go and have dinner in the centre . . .'

'Will you let me know if they look as if they're about to leave?'

'Only, I can't prevent them . . .'

'Just ring me . . . and thank you!'

He called Lucas.

'Listen carefully. This is important and delicate. You're going to go over to the Ritz with an inspector . . . Ask the concierge from me whether Ed Gollan is still in the bar . . . If he is, as I hope he will be, leave your partner in the lobby and go up to Gollan and his companion unobtrusively . . .

'No need to have your badge visible or to say the word "police" out loud . . . Tell him that it's about his car, that we need to ask him for some information, and insist that he follows you . . .'

'What about the woman. Do I bring her too?'

'Unless she's tall with dark hair, very beautiful, and called Mirella . . .'

Lucas squinted at the beers, the glasses still misted, then made to leave without a word.

'The main thing is, be quick . . . Drive at top speed . . .'

Although the beer was good, Maigret couldn't finish his sandwich. He was too restless to eat. Nothing stacked up in this case. He'd barely come up with a hypothesis when the facts contradicted it.

And, with the exception of the mysterious Stanley Hobson, they kept encountering individuals who appeared to be respectable.

He ended up calling Manessi, the auctioneer, at home.

'It's me again . . . . I hope I'm not interrupting a cocktail party . . . I am? . . . Then I'll be brief . . . Does the name Gollan mean anything to you? One of the top American experts? . . .'

He sighed several times as he listened to what Manessi was saying on the other end of the line.

'Yes . . . Yes . . . I should have expected it . . . One more question . . . I was told this afternoon that true art lovers buy and sell their paintings under the counter . . . Is that right? . . . I'm not asking you for names, of course . . . No! I'm not involved in an art case, or, if I am, it's unwittingly . . . One last thing . . . Is it possible that a man like Norris Jonker has fakes in his collection? . . .'

The reply was a guffaw.

'If he has, then so does the Louvre . . . It is true that some people claim that the *Mona Lisa* is a forgery . . .'

The door burst open. An excited, beaming Janvier waited impatiently for Maigret to finish his call to trumpet his news.

'Thank you . . . Go back to your guests . . . I might be wrong, but I think I may need you again . . .'

Janvier blurted out:

'This is it, chief! . . . We've found her . . .'

'Marinette?'

'Yes . . . Lagrume is bringing her back . . . He didn't break down, but apparently it's hard to find the Félix et Félicie inn in the dark . . . It's outside Pomponne, at the end of a mud track that's a dead-end . . .'

'Has she talked?'

'She swears she has no idea what happened . . . On hearing the shots, she immediately thought of Lognon . . . She was afraid they'd try to shoot her too . . .'

'Why?'

'She didn't explain . . . She made no objection to following Lagrume, except she asked to see his badge.'

She would be at Quai des Orfèvres within an hour at most. Meanwhile, if all went well, Ed Gollan would be there too, furious no doubt, threatening to call his embassy. It's crazy the number of people who invoke their embassy!

'Hello! . . . Yes . . . Speaking, dear Mr Pyke . . .'

The newly appointed chief inspector of Scotland Yard delivered his news without hurrying, apparently reading from a document in front of him and repeating each important piece of information.

Because there were some very important items. For example, concerning Mirella's divorce from her first husband, after only two years of marriage. It had been found that the fault lay with the young woman, on the grounds of adultery with no other than a certain Stanley Hobson.

Not only had the couple been caught in the act, in an insalubrious district of Manchester where Hobson had lodgings, but it had been established that the pair had been seeing one another throughout the two-year marriage.

'I could find no trace of Stanley in London during the following years. I hope to have that information for you tomorrow. Two of my men are contacting the people in Soho who know what's going on in those circles . . .

'One detail I almost forgot . . . Hobson is better known as Bald Stan . . . He lost his hair and his eyebrows at the age of twenty-three or twenty-four, as a result of some disease . . .'

Feeling hot, Maigret went to open the window a little, and he was busy draining one of the glasses of beer when he heard, in the corridor, someone speaking French with an American accent. He couldn't make out the words, but the tone of voice made it clear that the reluctant visitor was not happy.

That was why he put on his friendliest, most welcoming smile, and, as he opened the door, said:

'Do come in, Monsieur Gollan, and forgive me for disturbing you . . .'

7. Mirella's Choice

Ed Gollan had brown hair in a crew cut. Despite the cold, grey weather, he did not bother with an overcoat, and his lightweight suit without shoulder pads gave him an even more elongated shape.

He spoke in correct French, without fumbling for words, even though he was angry.

'This gentleman,' he said, pointing to Lucas, 'intruded on me in a particularly disagreeable manner, not only on me but on a lady who was with me . . .'

Maigret signalled to Lucas to leave the office.

'I apologize, Monsieur Gollan. If she is the person you are concerned about, you should know that inconveniences of this kind are part of her profession . . .'

His remark hit home.

'I presume this is about my car?'

'You are the owner of a yellow Jaguar, is that right?'

'I was.'

'What do you mean?'

'That I went to the police station of the first arrondissement this morning to report that it had been stolen.'

'Where were you last night, Monsieur Gollan?'

'At the residence of the Mexican consul, on Boulevard des Italiens.'

'Did you have dinner there?'

'In the company of a dozen people.'

'Were you still there at around ten o'clock?'

'Not only at ten o'clock but at two in the morning, as you will be able to verify.'

Spotting the tray with the beer and sandwiches, he looked surprised.

'I'd like you to tell me straight away . . .'

'One moment. I'm in a hurry too, more than you, believe me, but it is vital to proceed in an orderly manner. You left your car on Boulevard des Italiens?'

'No. You know better than I do that it is impossible to park there . . .'

'Where was it the last time you saw it?'

'Place Vendôme, where there are a number of parking spaces reserved for Ritz guests. I only had to walk a few hundred metres to my friend's residence.'

'You didn't leave his apartment?'

'No.'

'Did you receive a telephone call?'

He hesitated, taken aback by what Maigret knew.

'From a woman, yes.'

'A woman whose name you can't reveal, I presume? Would it not be Madame Jonker?'

'It could have been her, as a matter of fact I do know the Jonkers.'

'When you returned to the hotel, did you not notice that your car was no longer in its parking spot?'

'I used the Rue Cambon entrance, like most of the guests . . .'

'Do you know Stanley Hobson?'

'I am not inclined to be subjected to an interrogation, Monsieur Maigret, before being told what it is you believe I am mixed up in.'

'It so happens that some of your friends are in trouble . . .'

'Which friends?'

'Norris Jonker, for example . . . You have bought paintings from him and sold him paintings, I imagine?'

'I am not an art dealer . . . Museums and private collectors sometimes tell me they are looking for a painting by a specific artist, of special importance, from a specific period . . . If, during the course of my travels, I hear that such a painting is for sale, I merely mention it . . .'

'You don't take a commission?'

'That is none of your business. It is a matter for the tax authorities of my own country . . .'

'You have no idea, of course, who could have stolen your car? Was the key on the dashboard?'

'In the glove box. I'm absent-minded and it's the only way for me not to lose it.'

Maigret strained to hear the noises coming from the corridor and seemed to be conducting the interview reluctantly and without conviction.

This struck Gollan as somewhat surprising.

'I assume I can now go and rejoin the lady I have invited to dinner?'

'Not right away . . . I'm afraid I will need you again a little later . . .'

Maigret had heard footsteps, a door open and close again, and a woman's voice in the adjacent office. It was the evening of opening and closing doors as they would later dub it.

'Would you pop into my office for a moment, Janvier? It would be rude to leave Monsieur Gollan alone . . . We've made him miss his dinner, so if he wants a sandwich . . .'

The few inspectors who had been kept behind, including Lagrume, proud of his coup, darted curious looks at a charming young lady, dressed in a blue suit, who sat watching the goings-on around her.

'You're Detective Chief Inspector Maigret, aren't you? I've seen your photo in the newspapers. Tell me quickly whether he's dead . . .'

'No, mademoiselle Augier. He has been seriously wounded, but the doctors hope to save him . . .'

'Was it he who told you about me?'

'He's in no condition to talk, and won't be for some hours, if not for two or three days. Would you follow me?'

He showed her into a small office and shut the door.

'You'll understand, I think, if I tell you that we have little time. That's why I'm not asking you to go into details about what you know. I'll ask you all that later. For the moment, I have some questions for you. Was it you who informed Inspector Lognon that there were strange activities in the house opposite?'

'No. I hadn't noticed anything other than, at night, there was often a light on in the studio . . .'

'Where did he meet you?'

'In the street, as I was coming home. He told me that he knew which apartment I lived in and that he needed to spend two or three evenings at the window in order to watch someone. He showed me his police badge and his ID. I wasn't too happy about it and I almost called the police station . . .'

'What convinced you?'

'He looked unhappy. He told me that he had never had any luck, but that, if I helped him, all that would change because he was on to a very big case . . .'

'Did he say what it was?'

'Not the first evening.'

'Did you stay with him the first evening?'

'For a while, yes, in the dark. The curtains of the studio over the road didn't quite meet and, from time to time, you could see a man walk past holding a palette and brushes . . .'

'Dressed in white? With a towel around his head?'

'Yes. I joked that he looked like a ghost . . .'

'Did you see him painting?'

'Once. That evening, he had his easel in a part of the studio that we could see, and he was painting furiously . . .'

'What do you mean by painting furiously?'

'I don't know. I thought he seemed possessed . . .'

'Did you see other people in the studio?'

'A woman . . . She took her clothes off . . . Or rather he almost tore them off her . . .'

'Tall with dark hair?'

'It wasn't Madame Jonker, whom I know by sight.'

'Did you see Monsieur Jonker as well?'

'Not in the studio. In the studio I once saw a bald man, of a certain age . . .'

'What happened last night?'

'As on the other evenings, I went to bed early. I have a tiring job and the salon sometimes stays open very late, especially when there's a big ball or a gala . . .'

'Was Lognon in the living room?'

'Yes. We ended up becoming friends, the two of us . . . He never made a pass at me and he was very kind to me, like a father . . . He'd bring me chocolates or a bunch of violets to thank me . . .'

'Were you asleep at ten o'clock?'

'I was in bed, but I wasn't asleep yet. I was reading the newspaper . . . He knocked on my door . . . He was all worked up and told me that there was a development, that the painter had just been taken away, that it had all happened too quickly for him to have time to go downstairs . . .'

'"I'd better stay a little longer . . . It's likely that one of the men will return . . ."'

'He went back to the window and I fell asleep . . . The shots woke me . . . I looked outside . . . When I leaned out, I saw a body on the pavement . . . I had no idea what I was going to do yet, but I began to get dressed . . . The concierge came up and told me . . .'

'Why did you run away?'

'I thought that if the gangsters knew who he was and what he was doing in the building, they'd shoot me too . . . I still had no idea where I was going . . . I didn't think . . .'

'Did you take a taxi?'

'No. I walked down to Place Clichy and sat for a while in a café that was still open, where prostitutes looked me up and down . . . I remembered an inn I'd been to several times with a friend—'

'Jean-Claude, yes . . .'

'It was through him—'

'Look, mademoiselle. I am interested in everything that happened to you and I'd be delighted to hear the details of your escapade. But I have the feeling that there are more urgent matters. May I ask you, while you wait for me, to sit quietly in my inspectors' office, where I'm going to take you now . . . And while you're there, Janvier will take down your statement in writing . . .'

'Lognon wasn't mistaken?'

'No! Lognon knows his job and is rarely mistaken . . . As he told you, he's been unlucky . . . Either someone pulls the rug from under him, or he gets shot just as he was about to win the game . . . Come!'

He left her in the office next door and went back to Janvier in his own office.

'Take down the young lady's statement . . .'

Gollan, who was sitting down, leaped up.

'Have you brought her here?'

'It's not your lady friend, Monsieur Gollan, but a real lady . . . You still deny knowing Stanley Hobson, known as Bald Stan?'

'I do not have to reply.'

'As you wish . . . Sit down . . . You will perhaps learn something from the telephone conversation I am about to have . . . Hello! . . . Put me through to Monsieur Jonker, please . . . Norris Jonker, Avenue Junot . . .'

'Hello! Monsieur Jonker? . . . Maigret speaking . . . Since I left you, I have found the answer to a lot of the questions I asked you . . . The true answer, you understand? . . .

'For example, in my office I have Monsieur Gollan, who is not pleased to have been inconvenienced and who has still not found his car . . . A yellow Jaguar . . . The one that was parked outside your house at ten o'clock last night and that took away, among others, your lodger . . .

'I'm saying your lodger, yes . . . In a sorry state, apparently . . . Without any socks or shoes . . .

'Now listen to me, Monsieur Jonker . . . I could, later today or tomorrow morning, have you legally arrested for certain trafficking offences about which you know more than I do . . . I'm warning you that your house is under police surveillance, just in case . . .

'Please come here now, with Madame Jonker, to continue our conversation of this afternoon . . . If your wife were to make a fuss, tell her that we know her entire story . . . It is possible that, as well as Monsieur Gollan, she will meet here a certain Bald Stan—

'Be quiet, Monsieur Jonker, I'm doing the talking! It will be your turn to speak in a moment . . . It is unpleasant being mixed up in a forgery case, but it would be even more serious to be accused of being an accessory to murder, would it not?

'I am convinced that Inspector Lognon was shot without your knowledge, and probably without that of Monsieur Gollan . . . But I'm very much afraid that another crime is being planned, in which you would be more closely involved, because it concerns the man you kept locked up in your house . . . Where is he? . . . Tell me where he was taken and by whom . . . No! Not when you get here . . . Not in half an hour . . . Now, do you hear me, Monsieur Jonker?'

He heard the murmur of a woman's voice. Mirella must have been leaning over her husband. What was she advising him to do?

'I swear, Monsieur Maigret . . .'

'And I repeat that time is of the essence . . .'

'Wait! . . . I don't know the number off the top of my head . . . I need to look it up in my address book . . .'

Then Mirella interrupted:

'He's going to give you the address, Monsieur Maigret . . . He is Mario de Lucia, and he has a studio near the Champs-Élysées . . . Here's my husband . . .'

Jonker read:

'Mario de Lucia, 27A, Rue de Berri . . . He was the person who dealt with Frederico . . .'

'And Frederico is the painter who was working in your studio?'

'Yes . . . Frederico Palestri . . .'

'I'm expecting you, Monsieur Jonker . . . Don't forget to bring your wife.'

Maigret did not even look at the American critic. He was already picking up the phone again.

'Get me the police station of the ninth . . . Hello! . . . Who's speaking? . . . Dubois? . . . Take three or four men with you . . . And I mean three or four armed men, because the individual is dangerous . . . Get yourself over to 27A, Rue de Berri, and go up to the studio of a certain Mario de Lucia . . . If he's home, which is likely, arrest him, yes, despite the late hour . . .

'You'll find a man who's being held captive there, Frederico Palestri . . . I want both of them here as soon as possible . . . Once again, be careful! . . . Mario de Lucia is armed with a Mauser 7.63 . . . Find the weapon if he doesn't have it on him . . .'

He turned to Ed Gollan.

'You see, monsieur, that you were wrong to protest. It took me a long time to understand, because I am hardly familiar with the trafficking of artworks, genuine or fake . . . Furthermore, your friend Jonker is a gentleman who does not easily lose his cool . . .'

Once more, he grabbed the phone which had just rung.

'Yes . . . Hello! . . . Lucas? . . . Where are you? . . . Quai de la Tournelle? . . . Hôtel de la Tournelle? . . . I understand . . . He's eating in a café next door? . . . No, not on your own . . . Ask two neighbourhood inspectors to accompany you . . . After all, he could be the one who's playing with a large-calibre automatic . . . I'd be surprised, but what happened to poor old Lognon is quite enough . . .'

He walked over to the door of the inspectors' office.

'Get me a cold beer, would you . . .'

He came back and sat down at his desk, and filled a pipe.

'There you are, Monsieur Gollan! . . . I hope your painter is still alive . . . I don't know Mario de Lucia, but it is likely that he has a criminal record under one name or another . . . Otherwise, we'll contact the Italian police . . . We'll know in a few minutes . . . Admit that you are as anxious as I am . . .'

'I will only speak in the presence of my lawyer, Maître Spangler . . . His number is Odéon 1824 . . . No, I'm mistaken . . .'

'It doesn't matter, Monsieur Gollan . . . At this point,

I'm in no hurry to question you . . . It is a pity that a man like you should be mixed up in this case, and I hope that Maître Spangler will find some robust arguments in your defence . . .'

The beer still hadn't arrived when the telephone rang.

'Yes . . . Dubois? . . .'

He listened for a while without saying anything.

'Good! . . . Thank you . . . It's not your fault . . . Make your report directly to the public prosecutor . . . I'll drop by there later . . .'

Maigret stood up, refusing to respond to the American's questioning look. Gollan was pale.

'Has something happened? I swear that if . . .'

'Sit down and shut up.'

He went next door and signalled to Janvier, who was typing out Marinette Augier's statement, to follow him into the corridor.

'Something wrong, chief?'

'I don't know exactly what happened yet . . . The painter has been found hanged from the chain of the toilet in the bathroom where he was being held prisoner . . . Mario de Lucia has disappeared . . . You'll probably find his record upstairs . . . Put out a general alert to the stations, airports and borders . . .'

'What about Marinette?'

'She can wait . . .'

A couple was coming up the stairs, followed at a distance by a police officer from the eighteenth arrondissement.

'Please go into that room and wait for me, Madame Jonker . . .'

The two women, who knew one another by sight, had never found themselves in such close proximity, and they eyed each other with curiosity.

'And you, Monsieur Jonker, follow me . . .'

He took him into the small office where he had interviewed Marinette Augier.

'Have a seat . . .'

'Have you found him?'

'Yes.'

'Alive?'

The Dutchman no longer had his rosy complexion or his assurance. In the space of a few hours he had become an old man.

'Did de Lucia . . . kill him?'

'He was found hanged in the bathroom . . .'

'I've always said it would end badly . . .'

'For whom?'

'For Mirella . . . For the others . . . Especially my wife . . .'

'What do you know about her?'

It was hard to admit it, but he managed to, bowing his head.

'Everything, I think . . .'

'Nice and Stanley Hobson?'

'Yes.'

'What led up to the divorce from Herbert Muir in Manchester?'

'Yes.'

'Did you meet her in London?'

'At a country house on the outskirts of London, at the

home of friends . . . She was very popular in certain social circles . . .'

'And you fell in love with her? . . . Were you the one who suggested getting married?'

'Yes.'

'Did you already know?'

'It may sound unbelievable to you, but a Dutchman would understand . . . I hired a private detective to get information about her . . . I learned that she had lived with Hobson, known as Bald Stan, for several years, whom the British police had only managed to lock up once, for two years . . .

'He met up with her again in Manchester, when she was Mrs Muir . . . He didn't live with her in London but came to see her every so often to extort money from her . . .'

There was a knock at the door.

'You wanted a beer, chief?'

'You would probably rather have a brandy, Monsieur Jonker? . . . I'm sorry I can't offer you the tipple you drink at home . . . Someone bring me the bottle of brandy that's in my cupboard . . .'

They found themselves facing one another, and the brandy, downed in one, brought a little colour back into the Dutchman's cheeks.

'You see, Monsieur Maigret, I can't live without her . . . It is very dangerous to fall in love at my age . . . She told me that Hobson was blackmailing her, that she could get rid of him with a certain amount of money, and I trusted her . . . I paid up . . .'

'How did the paintings business begin?'

'You'll find it hard to believe me because you're not a collector . . .'

'I collect people . . .'

'I wonder how you'd classify me in your collection . . . Perhaps under fools? . . . Since you have investigated me, you have doubtless been told that I am a real expert on paintings of a certain period . . . When one has been passionate for so many years about a single thing, one ends up knowing a lot about it, doesn't one?

'I am often asked for my opinion of a painting . . . And it is enough for a work to have been part of my collection for its value to be undisputed . . .'

'To authenticate it, in other words . . .'

'That's what happens for all the great art lovers . . . As I told you when you came to my home, I sold some works in order to buy others, always rarer and more exquisite . . . Once you start, it is hard to stop . . . One day, I made a mistake . . .'

He spoke in a doleful voice, indifferent to what his fate might be.

'Even though it was a Van Gogh . . . Not one of those I had inherited from my father . . . A painting bought through a dealer and which I would have sworn was genuine . . . I kept it in my drawing room for a while . . . A South American art lover offered me a sum that allowed me to purchase a work I had been wanting for a long time . . .

'The deal was made . . . A few months later, a certain Gollan, whom I knew only by name, came to see me—'

'How long ago was that?'

'About a year . . . He spoke to me about the Van Gogh, which he'd had the opportunity to see at the home of my Venezuelan buyer, and he proved it was a skilful forgery . . .

'"I haven't said anything to your purchaser," he added. "It would be very unpleasant for you, would it not, if it became known that you'd sold a fake painting . . . Others who have bought paintings from you might become worried. Your entire collection would be under suspicion . . ."

'You are not a collector, I repeat . . . You have no idea what a blow this business was to me . . .

'Gollan came back to see me . . . One day, he told me he had discovered the author of the forgery, a brilliant boy, he claimed, just as capable of imitating a Manet as a Renoir or a Vlaminck . . .'

'Was your wife present during that conversation?'

'I don't recall . . . Perhaps it was I who told her about it afterwards? . . . Perhaps she encouraged me to accept what was being offered? . . . Perhaps I agreed of my own accord? . . . People say I am a wealthy man, but the word "wealth" is relative . . . While I can afford certain paintings, I don't have the means to buy others, no matter how tempting the opportunity . . . Do you understand?'

'What I think I understand is that there was a need for the forged paintings to pass through your hands so as to authenticate them beyond a doubt . . .'

'That's pretty much right . . . I displayed one or two fakes among my paintings and—'

'Just a moment! When were you introduced to Palestri?'

'A month or two later . . . Through Gollan, I had sold two of his works . . . Gollan preferred to sell them to South American art lovers or to small, little-known museums . . .

'Palestri was giving him cause for concern, because he was a kind of mad genius, and a sex maniac to boot . . . You guessed it on seeing his bedroom, did you not?'

'I began to understand when I saw your wife standing at the easel . . .'

'We had to pull the wool over people's eyes . . .'

'When and how did you find out that the goings-on in your house were being watched?'

'It wasn't me who noticed, it was Hobson . . .'

'Because Hobson had come back into your wife's life?'

'They both swear not . . . Hobson was a friend of Gollan's . . . He was the one who discovered Palestri . . . Are you managing to follow me? . . .'

'Yes . . .'

'I was caught in the spiral . . . I agreed to let him work in the studio, where no one would think to come looking for him . . . He slept in the bedroom you saw . . . He didn't ask to go out, on condition we procured women for him . . . Painting and women were his only passions . . .'

'I've been told he painted furiously . . .'

'Yes . . . We would place two or three masterpieces in front of him . . . He would circle them like a matador around a bull and, a few hours or a few days later, we would find a painting whose inspiration and execution were so identical that no one could distinguish between the two . . .

'He was a very unpleasant lodger . . .'

'Because of his demand for women?'

'And his coarseness. Even towards my wife . . .'

'Did he stop at just being crude?'

'I'd rather not know if he went too far . . . Perhaps . . . You saw the portrait he did of her with a few brush-strokes . . .

'One passion, Monsieur Maigret, is already a lot for a man, and I should have contented myself with my love of art and remained a reasonable collector . . . But I was fated to meet Mirella . . . Although none of this is her fault . . . What were you asking me?

'Oh! Yes . . . Who found out we were under suspicion? . . . It was a woman whose name escapes me, a striptease artist in a cabaret on the Champs-Élysées, I think, who de Lucia had brought for Palestri . . .

'The next day, she telephoned de Lucia to tell him she had been followed on leaving my house, then accosted by a strange man who had asked her all sorts of questions . . . De Lucia and Stan kept a watch on the neighbourhood . . . They noticed that, at night, a short, thin character prowled around Avenue Junot . . .

'Later, they saw him go into the building opposite with a young woman . . . He sat there in the dark, by the window, believing he couldn't be seen, but since he couldn't stop himself from smoking the occasional cigarette, the glow gave him away . . .'

'It didn't occur to anyone that he was from the police?'

'Stan Hobson said that if it was the police, the lookouts would work shifts . . . But it was always the same one, and he concluded that the man belonged to another gang, or that he was trying to find out enough to blackmail us . . .

'It became vital for Palestri to disappear from the house . . . De Lucia and Hobson dealt with it, last night, using Gollan's car . . .'

'Gollan knew about it, I presume?'

'Palestri refused to leave, convinced that having been used for nearly a year, he was going to be killed . . . He had to be knocked unconscious . . . He had already thrown his shoes into the garden . . .'

'Were you present?'

'No.'

'Your wife?'

'No! . . . We were waiting for him to be gone so we could clean up the studio and the bedroom . . . Stan had already taken away the frames and the painting he was doing the day before . . . What I can tell you, if I am still permitted to ask you to believe me, is that I was unaware of their intention to shoot the inspector . . . I only realized when I heard the gunfire . . .'

There was a long silence. Maigret was weary and he gazed with helpless sympathy at the aged man in front of him who was reaching tentatively for the brandy bottle.

'May I?'

Once the glass was empty, Jonker tried to smile.

'In any case, it's all over for me, isn't it? . . . I wonder what I'll miss most . . .'

His paintings, which had cost him so dear? His wife, about whom he had never had any illusions but needed so badly?

'You'll see, Monsieur Maigret, people won't believe that such an intelligent man can be so naive . . .'

He added, after a moment's thought:

'Except perhaps, collectors . . .'

In another office Lucas had begun interrogating Bald Stan.

For another two hours, there were comings and goings from room to room, questions, replies, the clacking of typewriters.

It was nearly one o'clock, like the night before, when the lights went out.

'I'll give you a lift home, mademoiselle . . . Tonight you can sleep in your bed without fear . . .'

They were in the rear of the taxi.

'Are you angry with me, Monsieur Maigret?'

'About what?'

'If I hadn't panicked and run away, wouldn't your job have been a lot easier?'

'We would have gained a few hours, but the result is the same . . .'

He did not seem so happy with that result, and even Mirella, when she was taken to the central police cells, had been the recipient of a look that was not devoid of sympathy.

Lognon left Bichat a month later, thinner than ever but with shining eyes because at the police station of the eighteenth arrondissement, he was a sort of hero. What was more, it was his photo, not Maigret's, that was in the newspapers.

The same day, he and his wife left for a village in the

Ardennes where the doctors had ordered him to conva-
lesce for two months.

Two months which, as Madame Maigret had foreseen,
he spent taking care of Madame Lognon.

Mario de Lucia had been arrested at the Belgian border.
Hobson and he had been sentenced to ten years' hard
labour.

Gollan denied all knowledge of the shooting in Avenue
Junot and got off with a two-year prison sentence for fraud.

Jonker only received one year, also for fraud, and,
because the months already spent in detention counted
double, he walked away from the court a free man.

. . . On the arm of his wife, because Mirella had been
acquitted for lack of proof.

Maigret, standing at the back of the courtroom, slipped
away quickly to avoid meeting them, especially since he
had promised to telephone Madame Maigret to tell her
the verdict.

The case was already history, because now it was June
and all people could talk about were the holidays.

INSPECTOR MAIGRET

OTHER TITLES IN THE SERIES

MAIGRET AND THE TRAMP
GEORGES SIMENON

'Maigret was devoting as much of his time to this case as he would to a drama keeping the whole of France agog. He seemed to be making it a personal matter, and from the way he had just announced his encounter with Keller, it was almost as if he was talking about someone he and his wife had been anxious to meet for a long time.'

When a Paris tramp known as 'Doc' is pulled from the Seine after being badly beaten, Maigret must delve into the past to discover who wanted to kill this mysterious figure.

Translated by Howard Curtis

INSPECTOR MAIGRET

OTHER TITLES IN THE SERIES

MAIGRET'S ANGER
GEORGES SIMENON

'There was a dressing table painted grey and cluttered with jars of cream, make-up, eyeliner. The room had a stale, faintly sickly smell. This was where the performers swapped their everyday clothes for their professional gear before stepping out into the spotlights, out to where men bought champagne at five or six times the going rate for the privilege of admiring them.'

Maigret is perplexed by the murder of a Montmartre nightclub owner, until he uncovers a crime much closer to home that threatens his own reputation.

Translated by Will Hobson

OTHER TITLES IN THE SERIES

And more to follow